THE UNWILLING VISCOUNT

LANDING A LORD

SUZANNA MEDEIROS

THE UNWILLING VISCOUNT
First Digital Edition: October 2022
First Print Edition: October 2022
Cover design © Kim Million
Edited by Victory Editing
ebook ISBN: 978-1-988223-19-3
Paperback ISBN: 978-1-988223-20-9

THE UNWILLING VISCOUNT

The Viscount Ashford has no immediate plans to wed. But with a mother determined to see him settled by the end of the Season, he must do what he can to salvage his freedom. Which leaves him with one choice—convince Miss Mary Trenton to accept his pretend suit. The woman he's come to think of as a friend is impervious to his charms, and that makes her the perfect choice for this pretend courtship.

Mary has no illusions that Ashford would look twice at her under normal circumstances. Agreeing to help him will allow her to experience what it is like to have a man pursue her. But somewhere along the way, while enjoying the gossip they're stirring, the line between fiction and reality becomes blurred.

Is it possible the attraction she's feeling for Ashford might be reciprocated?

To learn about Suzanna Medeiros's future books, you can sign up for her newsletter at https://www.suzannamedeiros.com/newsletter.

For Angelo Medeiros.

You were taken from us far too soon. You are loved and you are missed.
I look forward to the day we see each other again.

CHAPTER 1

March 1817

Viscount Ashford stood before his Mayfair town house and stared at the front door for almost a full minute. Dread settled over him at the thought of what awaited him on the other side of that door.

His mother.

She'd sent him a note last week to inform him she was coming to town for the season and that she intended to stay with him. He could only hope she didn't expect him to escort her to all the various entertainments.

The house had remained empty after his father's death several years ago, and he'd taken up residence last summer after returning to England following his time in the army. His mother normally stayed with one of his sisters when she was in town, but both Jane and Helen were now married and had households of their own.

He squared his shoulders and took a deep, calming breath. He'd faced his share of foes across the battlefield. Surely he could handle having his petite mother in residence for a few months.

The butler opened the door as soon as Ashford reached it. If Hastings had seen him hesitating outside the house, he gave no indication.

It was early evening, and he assumed his mother would be resting before dinner as was her custom. "Is Lady Ashford in her chambers?"

Hastings inclined his head. "Yes, my lord. Lady Benington is also here. She's waiting for you in the library."

Of course she was. Jane wouldn't miss the spectacle that was about to take place. At least his youngest sister, Helen, wasn't in town this spring. He was only slightly outnumbered.

He thanked the man and headed down the hallway to the library. He was delaying what he knew would be an uncomfortable meeting with his mother, but his sister would always be the lesser of two evils.

When he reached the room, Jane was standing near the window, looking out onto the back garden.

She turned as he entered, and one corner of her mouth quirked up in amusement. "I half feared you'd quit London. I'm happy to see Mother hasn't succeeded in driving you away. Not yet at any rate."

He fought to hold back a scowl as he waited for her to settle into a chair and then sank into the seat opposite her. As always, his sister was exquisitely dressed, and he didn't even have to ask if she'd be joining them for dinner. She wore a deep blue formal dress, and her light brown hair had been styled into ringlets around her face. Small blue jewels were sprinkled throughout the mass, which was swept up in an artful manner. If she planned to cajole him into accompanying her to a ball or rout that evening, she would be disappointed.

"Please tell me you're here to convince Mother to spend the next few months with you."

Jane let out a light laugh. "I'm already wed and have given her two grandchildren. Mother doesn't care what I do with my time. She's more interested in you and your pursuits."

He frowned. "If she's hoping one of those pursuits will be a wife, she's doomed to disappointment." It wasn't that he never wanted to wed, but it wasn't something he planned to do in the near future. When he married, it would be when he decided it was time.

"I don't know about that. Mother can be quite determined when she puts her mind to something."

He'd seen a hint of that strength the previous year when he'd visited her after resigning his commission and returning to England. Still, she couldn't have changed that much. The woman he'd known when he was a youth had deferred to her husband in all things.

"If she becomes unbearable, I'll find somewhere else to stay." He could just imagine the look on Lowenbrock's or Cranston's face if he turned up at one of their houses and asked them for shelter. He'd never hear the end of it, but they'd never abandon him in his hour of need.

"That won't dissuade our mother from carrying out her mission."

He let out a soft chuckle at the thought. "Are we talking about the same woman who used to cower whenever our father walked into a room? That woman never asserted herself a day in her life."

Jane's brows drew together at the memory. "Father was a tyrant, but I've come to see another side of our mother since his passing. She was very happy when you returned home and didn't want to press the matter when you visited her in Suffolk, but I fear her patience is at an end. She's set her mind on seeing you settled in the very near future."

"She can't force me to wed."

"She can try. She'll want you to be happily situated, of course, but be prepared to be subjected to a parade of England's most eligible young women over the next few months."

"Taking up residence elsewhere is looking more attractive." Or he could leave London altogether. He dismissed that idea almost as soon as it occurred to him. Cranston was in town, as was Lowenbrock and his new wife. He'd been looking forward to spending more time with the men who'd been his closest friends during the past few years of their fight against Napoleon. Certain he could manage his mother's attempts to marry him off, he wouldn't quit the battle-field so soon.

Jane lowered her voice and leaned forward in her chair. "You really don't want to leave Mother here all by herself."

Her words brought forth a pang of guilt that he did his best to ignore. "I know this is her first time staying in the house since Father passed, but I'm sure she'll be fine."

She arched a brow. "So you won't mind when she selects your future wife without any input from you and invites her to stay here? I'm sure she'll love telling everyone you've moved out of the town house to allow her time to get to know her future daughter-in-law."

He could only stare at his sister for several seconds, horror settling over him as he pictured that scenario playing out. After what felt like an eternity, he shook his head, but the image refused to leave his thoughts. "She wouldn't do that. And don't put the idea into her head."

"I wouldn't have to. Lady Herschel did that three years ago to force her reluctant son to wed."

He could actually feel the color drain from his face and found himself at a loss for words.

"So let me help you. I know a good number of suitable young women. We can have you betrothed by the end of the season without causing a scandal. Just tell me what type of woman you'd prefer."

He crossed his arms over his chest and scowled at his sister. "No, absolutely not. I have no intention of getting leg-shackled anytime soon."

"Which is precisely why I am here."

Ashford winced at the soft yet determined voice coming from the doorway and rose to his feet. After taking a moment to school his expression, he turned to face his mother.

The Dowager Viscountess Ashford swept into the room and engulfed him in a hug, the scent she'd favored since he was a boy wrapping around him. It threw him off-balance that his mother was now so effusive in showing affection. She'd always been reserved when he was younger, but that must have been for his father's benefit. Heaven knew the man had never liked him.

Despite the visible signs she was growing older, his mother was still a beautiful woman. When she pulled back, he couldn't help but notice the fine lines around her eyes and the lines that bracketed her mouth. Even her dark hair was becoming streaked with gray. But somehow those signs that she was no longer the flawless beauty he'd known growing up did nothing to diminish her appearance. She still looked beautiful in her lavender gown, a color he remembered her wearing often.

She clasped her hands at her waist and frowned up at him. "Now that's enough nonsense. You're almost thirty, and it's time for you to begin securing the family's future."

It took a great deal of effort to hold back his snort of amusement. "I was under the impression Father wanted Henry's children to inherit. That can still happen if I don't wed."

He'd long since come to terms with the fact that his father preferred his younger brother to him. If the previous Viscount Ashford could have declared Henry his heir, he would have done so long ago. His father had never come right out and said as much to him, but the man's constant criticism had made it clear.

That and the fact that his father hadn't cared when his heir declared his intention to enlist. His father had even gone out of his way to purchase him a commission the very next day.

His mother's lips pressed together in a firm line and she looked away, but not before he detected a hint of pain in her eyes. When she met his gaze again after several moments, it was as though she'd donned a mask.

"Your brother is not the Viscount Ashford. You are."

He lifted one shoulder in a shrug. "That doesn't mean he can't secure the line through his children."

"Henry won't be having children."

That was an odd statement. He opened his mouth to question her further, but Jane laid a hand on his arm to stop him. He met his sister's gaze, and she shook her head. There was definitely something here that neither his mother nor his sister wanted to talk about. Had his brother had an accident that rendered him incapable of performing sexually? He winced inwardly at the thought and let the subject drop.

His mother moved to his side and took his arm. "We can discuss this further over dinner," she said as she turned them toward the door. "I've been told you haven't even looked at the invitations you've received. Now that I'm here, I'll handle matters and ensure you're seen at only the most sought-after events. Your wife must be a woman of impeccable breeding. I'll start making inquiries in the morning as to which families are in town."

He cast a pleading glance at his sister, hoping she would say something to curtail his mother's determination.

Instead, Jane smiled at him and joined forces with their mother. "I've already started a list. We can compare notes."

CHAPTER 2

Mary Trenton thanked the young footman who helped her into her sister's carriage. She waited for him to close the door before sinking back into the cushions and closing her eyes. A sigh of relief escaped when the vehicle finally began moving and she willed her unsettled nerves to calm. Everything would be better soon because she was on her way to see her friend Amelia.

To say the past week… no, the past month… had been trying would be a vast understatement. Ever since Amelia had written to let Mary know she and her new husband, the Marquess of Lowenbrock, would be in London for the season and to beg Mary to join them in town.

Spring and early summer had always been Mary's favorite time of the year. That became truer when circumstances forced her to move in with her sister

Edwina after their parents died in a carriage accident. Every spring, when her sister departed for London, Mary could feel the tension with which she lived on a daily basis leaving her body. With her sister away for the season, Mary was free from her constant surveillance and criticism.

That all changed with the arrival of Amelia's letter. Edwina had been annoyed when Mary asked to accompany her and Lord Fairbanks to London. Mary was no fool, however. She knew Edwina would deny the request and so she'd casually dropped the one piece of information that would change her sister's mind. The news Mary had held back for just such an occasion. The fact that her friend was now the Marchioness of Lowenbrock.

After learning that Amelia Weston was now a marchioness, her sister's displeasure had vanished. Mary wasn't taken in by her sister's false smiles, knowing it meant her sister planned to ingratiate herself and her husband into Lowenbrock's circle of friends. That was the only reason Edwina had allowed Mary to accompany them to London.

That hadn't stopped her sister from dropping her customary snide comments and criticisms into their conversations. Edwina was incapable of holding back altogether and was on her best behavior only when Lord Fairbanks was present.

Today Mary would finally see her friend again, and she was dismayed to be running late. Because of course her sister had taken so long to send the carriage back after taking it out for her own errands.

The trip to Amelia's residence was a short one, and Mary realized she could have walked the distance. She'd have to get a maid to show her the route for her future visits.

The carriage slowed to a halt, and a footman opened the door to help her down. She barely had time to take in the facade of the imposing town house that was Amelia's London home when the front door opened and her friend was rushing down the steps. They met in the middle of the short walk that set the house back from the street and embraced.

"I feared you weren't coming," Amelia said when she pulled back.

Mary rolled her eyes. "That would be Edwina's doing. She's out today, visiting, and assured me she would send the carriage back for me on time. She either forgot or she did it on purpose."

She could have kicked herself when she saw the way Amelia's forehead creased in concern. Knowing how her friend worried about her, she shouldn't have said anything.

Mary laced her arm through Amelia's and turned them toward the house. "Let's not worry about her right now. You need to show me your home."

Amelia smiled up at her. "It's hard to believe I'm now mistress here."

Her friend's words surprised her. "You weren't

before? Your uncle never married, and so I just assumed you were."

Amelia turned to the butler when they entered the house and asked for tea to be brought to the drawing room. When she looked at Mary again, her smile held a hint of sadness. "I haven't been back here since Uncle fell ill, and I wasn't yet of age the last time we were in residence."

Mary followed Amelia into the drawing room and took a seat next to her on the settee. "But you were in London last summer?" Amelia hadn't told her the details about what had happened after she'd left her uncle's manor in Yorkshire and returned to London. She'd assumed her friend had stayed here.

Amelia nodded. "I stayed briefly with John's sister, Louisa, but I didn't want to impose. After that I spent some time with a trusted friend of the family. Since John was the new marquess, this house wasn't mine to do with as I wished."

Mary wanted to press for details, but one look at her friend's face told her Amelia didn't want to discuss the matter further. She'd known that Amelia was sad when they'd left Yorkshire together, but apparently there had been more to her sorrow than just being homesick, which Mary had assumed was the only issue at the time.

"Oh good, the tea is here," Amelia said.

Mary let out a small sigh as a footman brought in their refreshments and set the tray on the table before the settee. "Fine, I'll change the subject. But I want to hear all about it soon. It's clear you've been holding out on me."

Amelia smiled. "There is one bit of news I can share right now." She leaned in a little closer and lowered her voice. "John and I are expecting. Come the fall, I'll be a mother!"

Mary let out a small laugh and engulfed her friend in a quick hug. She cast a look at Amelia's belly. Her friend wore a pale yellow morning gown that had settled close to her body when she sat, but Mary couldn't detect even a hint of her friend's pregnancy. "There is no sign yet that you're increasing?"

Amelia shook her head, the dark curls that framed her face bouncing with the movement. "Not yet, and we haven't announced it. John's family knows, but I don't know if he's told his friends. And I wanted to tell you in person."

Mary could only stare at Amelia in wonder, taking in the glow of happiness that seemed to light her from within. "I'm so happy for you, and for Lord Lowenbrock, of course."

"I thought my time had passed for such things. With no chance of having a season—and let's face it, I would have been too old in any case—I had little hope of marrying."

"And to someone who clearly loves you as much as you love him."

Mary had visited Amelia in Yorkshire again in the

fall for their wedding. That time the marquess's sisters had brought their children, and the house had been filled with the sounds of happiness. It had struck her just how different it was from the cold, quiet emptiness of the house she shared with her sister and brother-in-law. No children had blessed their marriage, but she imagined there was still time for Edwina and Lord Fairbanks.

From the way the marquess had gazed at Amelia, it was obvious to everyone that he cared for her. And once they'd wed, he hadn't even tried to hide his affection. Mary's visit hadn't been long—despite the respite from the tedium of living under her sister's ever-watchful gaze, she knew her life would only be more unpleasant if she extended the visit. For some reason, Edwina seemed intent on ensuring Mary was as unhappy with her lot in life as she was.

"I've been very fortunate." A strange light entered Amelia's eyes then as her gaze narrowed. Mary only had a moment to wonder what had caused it when her friend spoke again. "You and Ashford make a lovely pair. I didn't miss the fact you danced a waltz during the ball we held."

Mary couldn't hold back her peal of laughter. Clearly her friend was determined to matchmake.

Amelia folded her arms across her chest as she waited for Mary's laughter to fade. Finally, impatient, she said, "I wasn't the only one to notice. People couldn't stop whispering when it was clear the two of you were enjoying yourselves immensely."

Mary smiled, remembering that evening with great fondness. "So our ruse was successful?"

One of Amelia's brows lifted. "Ruse?"

"Of course. It was all pretend. As soon as Lowenbrock announced that you and he were betrothed, every eye in the room turned to Ashford. Many had come to ensnare a marquess for their daughters that evening, and when he was no longer available, they decided a viscount would do just as well. It was quite comical."

Amelia sighed as she turned to the tray and poured out their tea. "John did say something about Ashford being put out that he wasn't given warning about the announcement."

"He wasn't happy. I'm sure he would have fled from the ballroom if he'd known it was coming."

She took her teacup from Amelia as another small laugh escaped. The poor man had felt like prey. He'd been amused as he watched guests young and old parade before Lowenbrock as they tried to gain his attention, but the evening had quickly lost its appeal when all that interest turned to him.

"I still think the two of you would make a good match," Amelia said.

Mary shook her head. "He would never be interested in me. I'm too ordinary for someone like him."

"Nonsense." Amelia waved a hand in dismissal.

"I am plain. My hair isn't fair, but neither is it that rich shade of dark brown that does wonders against your fair skin. My eyes are too big and are an ordinary shade of brown, and my mouth too wide. According to Edwina, the latter is unseemly, though I can't imagine why."

Amelia let out an indelicate snort at her last statement. Mary took the teacup from her friend's hands as Amelia coughed into a napkin.

She placed their cups on the table before turning back to her friend, confused by her reaction. "Did I say something amusing?"

Now it was Amelia's turn to laugh, leaving Mary even more confused.

Amelia turned in her seat and grasped Mary's hands. "I suppose your mouth could be seen as unseemly."

Mary let out a small huff of annoyance. She tried to pull her hands away, but Amelia's grasp only tightened.

"Your sister is jealous of you, and it seems she has convinced you that no man would find you attractive."

"Jealous?" Mary shook her head. "Of what, my too-wide mouth?" Mary shook her head. "That is preposterous. She has the appearance of a delicate Staffordshire figure while I—"

"Look like sin itself."

Mary's mouth snapped closed and Amelia continued.

"Lady Fairbanks is, indeed, quite lovely, but it is a cold thing. Men like a little warmth in their women. You sell yourself short." Amelia let out a sigh and released Mary's hands. "We'll have to keep a close eye on you. I'm shocked at how many men have propositioned me, assuming it no small thing that I would be unfaithful to my husband. But you…" She shook her head.

"My too-wide mouth, and I thank you for trying to make me feel better."

Amelia could only shake her head, but her eyes continued to spark with amusement.

"Clearly I lack knowledge in this matter that you now possess." She pondered the mystery for several seconds before the truth struck her. Amelia was now a married woman and so had experience that she lacked. Mary didn't want to ask the next question, but she needed to know. She squared her shoulders. "Does it have to do with…?" Despite her attempt at bravado, she couldn't quite bring herself to continue.

Amelia let out a breath. "The bedchamber and what happens there between a husband and wife. Yes. Although it could happen in any room in the house—"

Shocked, Mary placed a hand over her friend's mouth. "That is more than enough information, thank you very much. I really don't want to think about what you and Lowenbrock have been up to while attempting to conceive his heir." Her mouth twisted as she tried to banish those thoughts from her mind.

Amelia smiled. "Fair enough. But trust me, there will be men who seek your attention. And given that you are no longer a young woman, many of them won't be looking for a wife but a mistress."

Well, that was a wonderful thought. Her parents had passed away before she'd had her first season, and she'd had to go live with her sister. All talk of finding her a husband had ceased at that point. She hated the idea of being approached by men who wouldn't even offer her the benefit of marriage. Why would any woman bother?

"At any rate," Amelia said, breaking into her thoughts, "you must stay for dinner. John mentioned that Lord Ashford and Lord Cranston might be joining us, and it will be a great opportunity to become reacquainted."

Mary let out a sigh. "You're matchmaking."

"Of course not." Amelia looked away, unable to meet her gaze as she told the blatant lie.

"It will come to naught. Lord Ashford and I shared one dance to keep all the young, hopeful women from descending on him. But…"

Amelia's gaze swung back to meet hers. "But what?"

Mary couldn't hold back her amusement. With a

laugh, she squeezed one of Amelia's hands and shook her head. "You are incorrigible. I was merely going to say that I would love to join you for dinner. Lord Fairbanks and my sister will be going out tonight, so it was going to be just me alone at the house."

Amelia's brows drew together.

"*That* was just how I wanted it. Lord Fairbanks mentioned I was welcome to join them, but I knew Edwina wouldn't be pleased. And honestly, I'm sure there will be more than enough opportunity to attend similar events. I was hoping to spend more time with you today."

"You know me so well," Amelia said.

Mary watched her friend as she leaned forward and placed a chocolate-covered sweet on a plate and handed it to her before taking one for herself. "I figured at the very least you owe me one dinner after enticing me from my peaceful solitude in the country."

She took a bite of the small confection and let out a moan of appreciation. Her sister had put on weight after her marriage to Lord Fairbanks and had banned all sweets from the house. Her gaze swung to the serving tray, and she was dismayed to find there were only a few more sweets on it.

Amelia must have realized she planned to snatch the rest. "Don't even think about it. I'm eating now for two, so you can't take the rest."

Mary let out a huff of disappointment. "Fine, but

you have to promise to have more of these the next time I visit."

Amelia laughed as she placed two more chocolate confections on their plates. "I think I can accommodate your request."

CHAPTER 3

The day's session at the House of Lords had run late again. Evening had descended, and Ashford gladly accepted Lowenbrock's invitation to dinner. Cranston was also joining them, which was a minor miracle since the man spent most nights in a different woman's bed.

In the past they would have gone to a tavern, but Lowenbrock—Ashford still had a difficult time thinking of his friend John Evans as the Marquess of Lowenbrock—was a married man now, and it was almost impossible to tear him away from his wife's side. Ashford didn't complain, however. The marchioness was good company, and anything was better than being subjected to another disastrous evening.

His mother and sister had made good on their threats to find him a wife. His mother had only just arrived in town, and she'd already dragged him to a ball last night—the first of many, he'd been assured. He'd wanted to believe the evening wouldn't be intolerable. It wouldn't be like the ball he'd attended last summer at Lowenbrock's manor when he'd become the center of attention after his friend had announced his betrothal. He'd hated every second of it.

Well, not every second. Thank goodness Mary Trenton had been there. Their families had been acquainted, and she'd helped him to keep the fortune hunters at bay. He hadn't thought he needed rescuing now that he was in London since there were plenty of titled, unwed men in town.

Any comfort he'd derived from those thoughts was swept away by his mother's and his sister's determination to find him a bride. Every time he'd managed to escape the stifling crowds, he'd come face-to-face with his mother, who dragged him off to meet yet another young woman.

And deuced if she didn't do it right before a new set was about to start, all but forcing him to ask the woman to dance.

He'd intended to remain around the fringes of the room, surrounded by other men who were there against their will. And if he was very lucky, he'd thought he might be able to escape to a card room.

That morning, his mother hadn't been pleased when he'd told her he wouldn't be escorting her to whatever entertainment she planned to attend.

Apparently the parents of one of the women with whom he'd danced last night—he couldn't for the life of him remember which one—was hosting a musicale. His mother's presence in town was already suffocating him.

Lowenbrock escorted them to his study when they arrived at his town house. Ashford accepted the brandy his friend offered him.

"Is this now my life? People pressing me on all sides to wed?" He downed the drink in one long swallow.

Lowenbrock took his glass but, instead of refilling it, set it aside. Ashford scowled at the man.

Cranston clapped him on the shoulder. "You should enjoy yourself. Surely you can find a nice widow with whom to entertain yourself over the season."

Ashford dropped into a chair, not caring that his friends were looming over him. "That's not going to happen with my mother standing watch over me."

Cranston winced.

"I blame the two of you for my misery," Ashford said, ignoring their amused glances at one another.

Lowenbrock set aside his own half-finished glass. "If you hate us so much, you should beg off dinner and go find better company. I'll explain to Amelia that you were called away."

Ashford shuddered at the thought. He was much safer here than returning home. He supposed he could find something else to do, but for some reason he wanted to spend the evening with his friends. Even if they were amused by his situation.

There was a soft knock at the door before Lowenbrock's wife let herself into the room. His friend went to her side and dropped a kiss on her cheek before turning to them again, a large smile on his face.

"I hope you don't mind having these ruffians join us this evening?"

Amelia greeted them with a curtsy. "It is always a pleasure. Dinner will be served soon, and we'll be having another guest."

Ashford found himself tensing and had to will his muscles to relax. Surely his friend's wife wasn't joining in on the quest to find him a wife.

"Miss Mary Trenton visited me today and will be joining us for dinner."

Ashford wanted to sag with relief. Miss Trenton was here. Her sharp wit would be just what he needed to distract him from his current troubles.

"It will be just like last summer, when we were all together at Brock Manor," Cranston said, his tone light with amusement.

Ashford found himself smiling and ignored the way Cranston's eyes landed on him with speculation. He'd already dealt with prodding from the man after dancing a waltz with Miss Trenton at Lowenbrock's ball. If Cranston was trying to get a rise out of him now, he would be disappointed.

"Where is Miss Trenton now?" Lowenbrock asked.

"I left her in the library when one of the footmen informed me of your arrival. She's promised to join us in the drawing room."

Ashford let out a soft chuckle at that, and everyone turned to look at him. "Surely I'm not the only one who remembers how she'd spend hours in the library at Brock Manor. I seem to remember you having to send someone to drag her away on several occasions so she could join us for dinner."

Lady Lowenbrock smiled at the memory. "We'll have to see whether history will repeat itself tonight."

She took her husband's arm, and together they made their way down the hall. "I hope you don't mind that we're not being formal tonight. You're all part of our extended family here."

Ashford let out a small laugh. "That will be a welcome relief."

Lady Lowenbrock's smile dimmed. "John mentioned that your mother is in town. Does Lady Ashford insist on formality for each meal?"

He raised one shoulder in a shrug. "To an extent, she does, yes. But the real issue is the fact that she is on a quest to find me a wife."

They'd just arrived at the drawing room, and the sound of Miss Trenton's laughter indicated she'd overheard his statement.

"I can assure you this is no laughing matter," he said with a small bow.

He met her amusement with all the seriousness he could muster in the face of her amused countenance. Damn but it was good to see her again. Here, finally, was one woman he wasn't related to, or who wasn't already wed, who didn't have marital designs on him.

"I can only imagine how trying it must be, having beautiful young women hanging on your every word and going out of their way to please you. It must be a great hardship."

Cranston let out a bark of laughter at her jab. "I don't know why he's complaining. The attention is quite pleasant."

Mary didn't say anything when she met his gaze, but Ashford could see that she wanted to gloat about being correct in her assessment of the situation.

"I can assure you that being under the watchful gaze of my mother and older sister is not at all enjoyable."

Lady Lowenbrock gave him a sympathetic smile. "Well, you can enjoy yourself here without worrying we've placed any expectations on you."

"I shall savor the experience since I imagine my evenings will soon be occupied with the business of trying to avoid matchmaking mamas—my own included."

John clapped him on the shoulder with an exaggerated wince. "I don't envy you. That one ball where everyone's attention was on me was more than enough to last a lifetime."

Ashford's gaze met Miss Trenton's, and he could see she was remembering that evening as well, along with his desperate plea for her assistance. With any luck, he might be able to call on her again in the future.

CHAPTER 4

It was late morning when a footman found her in the library. Mary glanced at the white card he held aloft on a silver tray, but she already knew it would have Amelia's name on it.

They'd arranged to visit the modiste today. Mary's dresses were fine for the country, but they were out of date. When she'd tried to explain why she couldn't attend all the evening entertainments to which Amelia wanted to drag her, her friend had insisted Mary allow her to buy her a few new dresses.

Mary wasn't comfortable with the idea of Amelia arranging for an entire wardrobe. She did have some money set aside, a small amount left to her by her parents for a dowry as well as a small yearly stipend. She knew it was unlikely she'd ever wed, and since she hadn't needed to touch any of her allowance in the years since her parents' passing, she intended to pay

Amelia back the money they'd be spending today. She had no doubt that her friend's offer was genuine, but Mary didn't want to take advantage of Amelia's generosity.

When she reached the drawing room, she wasn't surprised to hear her sister's voice floating out into the hallway. Edwina was ever the opportunist, and she wouldn't miss this chance to ingratiate herself with the new Marchioness of Lowenbrock.

Mary swept into the room and, aware of her sister's eyes on her, hugged her friend. She took a step back before saying, "I see you have already met my sister, Baroness Fairbanks."

Amelia smiled at Edwina. "Yes, she has made me feel welcome."

"Any friend of my sister's is always welcome here." Edwina's smile was stretched to an almost unnatural width.

Mary resisted the urge to roll her eyes at Edwina's obvious attempts at flattery. She could almost see the wheels turning in her sister's head. No doubt Edwina was imagining how she could sweep in and become Amelia's new best friend. But her sister didn't realize that Amelia was that rare being among the ton—a loyal friend.

"I was just telling Lady Fairbanks that we're visiting the modiste today."

"And I was just about to tell Lady Lowenbrock that I would be very happy to accompany you."

Of course she would. Mary's own smile felt tight as she faced her sister. "I thought you were planning to visit Lady Dalrymple?" Of course, the woman was merely a baroness like Edwina. Her sister would throw aside that acquaintance like last year's fashions for the chance to become friends with Amelia.

Edwina couldn't quite hide her exasperation, but she kept her smile in place. "I'm sure she'll understand—"

"Oh no," Amelia said with just the right amount of sincerity. "Please don't change your plans on my behalf."

Edwina's smile dimmed. "I would be delighted to show you around. You're new to London, are you not?"

"I am, yes. But my sisters-in-law will be joining us afterward. They've taken me under their wing and, by extension, Mary." She beamed in Mary's direction.

Which was her cue to deliver the killing blow. Edwina never paid attention to what Mary had to say, so she was certain she had no idea who Amelia now counted as family. "Oh yes, Lady Overlea and Lady Kerrick are delightful. I met them last summer when I visited Amelia in Yorkshire."

Mary delighted in the way her sister's mouth tightened when she realized that Mary would be spending the morning with two marchionesses and a countess. Her smile had dropped entirely, but somehow she'd managed to keep from frowning. Which, in Mary's opinion, must have taken an act of extraordinary will. Her sister was never one for hiding her displeasure.

Still, she wasn't about to give up. "It will be no hardship…"

"Please don't let us put you out," Amelia said. "I'm sure we'll have the opportunity to become better acquainted soon, but for now we must be going. I was already late when I left the house this morning, and if we don't hurry, we'll miss our appointment with Madame Argent."

The name meant nothing to Mary, but clearly it did to Edwina because she looked as though Amelia had kicked her in the stomach. Which could only mean that the person who would be making Mary's gowns was above her sister's reach.

Mary hoped she would be able to pay Amelia back soon for her kindness, although it might take her longer than she'd expected.

Knowing that their window of opportunity to escape was short, Mary linked arms with Amelia and led her from the house. She could almost feel her sister's glare boring holes in the back of her head.

"We must hurry," Mary said, her voice pitched low.

Amelia shot her a curious glance but didn't argue. When they were seated in the carriage and pulling away from the town house, Mary finally felt the tension begin to leave her body.

Amelia leaned against Mary, allowing their shoulders to bump. "You act as though Lady Fairbanks was going to force her way into the carriage." At Mary's nod, her mouth dropped open for a moment before she snapped it closed again. "I know she wasn't pleased, but surely she wouldn't have…"

Mary let out an indelicate snort. "If we had tarried a moment longer, it would have been a very real possibility. And since you're much too kind-hearted to have her tossed back onto the street…" She shuddered. "It would have been horrible."

Amelia sighed. "I hope I haven't made things worse between the two of you."

"I'm sure you haven't. Edwina ignores me most of the time. And she wouldn't dare do anything that would reflect badly on her." Mary shrugged. "No, she'll save that for later, when we return to the country."

Amelia bit her lip. "Perhaps I should invite her and Lord Fairbanks to dinner one evening."

Mary cringed as she imagined the way her sister would crow after receiving the invitation. "Please don't invite Lowenbrock's family. Edwina will be insufferable enough bragging to all her friends that she's now friends with the Marchioness of Lowenbrock and her handsome husband. I wouldn't want your sisters-in-law to be taken in by her flattery."

Amelia patted her knee. "You needn't fear about that. You've met Catherine and Louisa. John's sisters are levelheaded and are unlikely to be taken in by honeyed words."

Mary nodded in reply, but she couldn't help the twinge of fear that went through her. What if Edwina was genuinely nice to everyone but her? Her sister did have friends in town, after all, so she wasn't always hateful.

Which would mean that perhaps there was something unlikeable about Mary. She tried to push the unwelcome thought from her mind, knowing that to entertain it further would be to play right into her sister's hands. For some reason Edwina had painted her as the villain their entire lives, and the distance between them only worsened when their parents died and Mary had gone to live with her and Baron Fairbanks. She didn't know why her sister disliked her so much, but she refused to give her the satisfaction of sowing doubt into her friendships.

She changed the subject to her friend's writing. She'd known that Amelia was working on a novel but hadn't realized it had been published.

Her mouth dropped open when Amelia told her she was the author of *A Fallen Lady*.

"I will give you a copy of course. I wanted to tell you the moment the book was accepted but didn't want to risk your sister learning that information."

Mary closed her mouth with a snap. "Edwina's been talking about that novel. She says it's quite scandalous and that everyone is trying to discover the author's identity."

Amelia's smile held more than a hint of amusement. "I know. I can't tell you how many people have approached me with the most outlandish theories about the author."

Mary shook her head in amazement. She'd always thought her friend was talented, but pride filled her at Amelia's accomplishment.

The trip to Bond Street passed quickly as Amelia told her about how the novel's opening scene was based on her first meeting with her husband. She'd been working as a barmaid one evening as research for her book, and he'd come to her rescue when one of the patrons had gotten a little too friendly.

Which meant that when she returned home and realized the man who had saved her that evening was none other than her uncle's long-sought heir, she'd spent the first few weeks of their acquaintance dressed in frumpy clothing and wearing her reading glasses to hide her identity whenever she was in his presence.

Amelia had her in stitches when the carriage slowed to a halt. They thanked the footman who helped them down, and Mary followed her friend.

They entered the modiste's store to the sound of delicate bells chiming. The air was perfumed with an exotic scent that somehow enticed the senses without being overwhelming.

"My lady." A very pretty woman with dark hair

greeted them with a deep curtsy. Her accent identified her as French, and Mary could only assume this was the modiste. The woman's hair was jet black, the slight lines around her eyes the only sign she was older than she appeared. "I did not realize you would be visiting my humble store today. I will turn the sign so we won't be disturbed…"

"There will be no need," Mary said. "We are only here to purchase one or two gowns. I don't want you to turn away any customers on my behalf."

Madame Argent froze at her words. Mary waited while the woman looked her up and down. If the modiste thought to intimidate her, she would have to try harder. Edwina's criticisms had long since inured her to the censure of others.

"Of course, if you're too busy to accommodate Miss Trenton, we can always go elsewhere…" Amelia began.

"*Non*, I will not hear of it." Her smile widened, and she twirled one finger in the air.

With a sigh, Mary rotated in place and braced herself for the inevitable criticisms.

"*Mon dieu*, her clothing is quite out of date. Who has been dressing her?"

"Clearly no one as talented as you," Amelia said.

Madame Argent took the compliment as her due. "That goes without saying, *non*? But never mind, I shall take her on." She took hold of Mary's dress and pulled it back to reveal the curves hiding beneath the loose fabric that gathered just below her bosom. "Oh yes, I can do much here. I don't know why you are hiding your figure, *ma cherie*, but together we will unearth it."

The modiste snapped her fingers at another woman, who approached and started flitting about, taking Mary's measurements while the modiste watched them with narrowed eyes.

Mary turned to her friend, who was looking through a book that she assumed contained dress designs. In that moment, Amelia seemed every inch a marchioness.

Her friend looked up and caught Mary watching her. "What is it?"

Mary shook her head. "What happened to the shy, studious young woman I used to know?"

Amelia grinned back at her. "Oh, she's still here. If I take off my gloves, you'll find that my fingers are covered with ink stains."

"Still, you've taken to your new role as though you were born to it."

The seamstress stepped away and brought the measurements to the modiste. They consulted together in the corner, their voices low.

Amelia continued, her voice lowered as well. "John's sisters have taught me a thing or two. It is amazing how much people are willing to bend over backward to help you when they know they'll be rewarded handsomely."

Mary winced at the reminder. “I don’t have very much money to spend. Perhaps enough for one ball gown and two day dresses—”

Amelia waved a hand in dismissal. “You have done me a great favor in agreeing to come to London to keep me company and giving up your free time away from your sister. And since I’m dragging you around, I insist on providing you with a few gowns. All in the name of helping me to acclimate to my new position in society.”

Mary felt a pang of guilt. “You have Lady Overlea and Lady Kerrick here to help you.”

Amelia’s mouth turned down at the corners. “Yes, but I *want* to do this for you.”

She let out a sigh. “You’re still intent on matchmaking.”

Amelia grasped her hands and gave them a quick squeeze. “Can you blame me? I want the same happiness for you that I’ve found.”

Mary would be lying if she said she didn’t want that herself, but she couldn’t ignore the small voice inside her that tried to remind her she was too old to be on the marriage mart.

When she realized that voice sounded exactly like her sister’s, her refusal died, unspoken. What would it hurt to allow herself this one last chance to find happiness? “I don’t want to take advantage of your generosity.”

Amelia smiled at her. "Please allow me to do this for you."

"What if Lord Lowenbrock—?"

"John is of the same mind. It hasn't been all that long since he and his sisters had very little money and even fewer prospects. He hasn't forgotten that feeling. He wants to help you as much as I do."

They'd spoken about her. She waited for the customary feeling of embarrassment to wash over her, but it never came. She realized that was because she trusted Amelia and her husband. The thought that they'd been talking about her didn't leave her with the same discomfort as the knowledge that Edwina spoke about her with Lord Fairbanks. Edwina was careful in her criticisms, of course, because her husband was very circumspect in his duty in caring for his sister-in-law, but Mary still waited for the day they told her she was no longer welcome in their home.

Madame Argent clapped her hands together as she approached. "A full wardrobe, *non?*"

Mary shook her head. "One ball gown and two day dresses—"

"Yes, a full wardrobe," Amelia said.

Mary turned to her friend. "That is too much…"

"Nonsense," the modiste said. "A woman of your beauty should shine. When I am finished, everyone will know your name."

"And yours as well," Amelia said.

Madame Argent inclined her head. "That is without question."

"Before we begin, I wanted to mention that there is a ball tomorrow night, and I'd like very much for Miss Trenton to accompany us."

"So soon?" Mary asked. She'd assumed she would have some time to acclimate herself to the idea of going out in public. And to brace herself for Edwina's displeasure at seeing Mary at the same events she was also attending.

Madame tsked. "That is very short notice, and I do have a number of other clients…"

"Perhaps I should skip the ball tomorrow. I can wait for the dresses to be finished."

Amelia took her hand and turned to face the seamstress. "I had my heart set on showing off my friend. Perhaps you can alter one of the dresses you were making for me. The white silk? We are of a similar height, I'm sure it wouldn't be too much trouble."

Madame's eyes dipped over her figure, then back to Amelia's, no doubt thinking the same thing as Mary.

"I am not as well-endowed as you," she said.

Heat colored her friend's cheeks. "I'm sure it wouldn't be too difficult to take in the bodice a little. I am not *that* much larger than Miss Trenton."

Mary did not have to give voice to her opinion of her friend's suggestion.

Amelia's eyes narrowed. "Or we could pad your corset."

Mary let out a bark of laughter at that. "We most certainly will not. Edwina would just love to make a comment in front of all her friends about the sudden growth I seem to have experienced at my very advanced age."

"It will be no trouble at all," Madame said, breaking into their conversation, no doubt afraid that Mary would talk her friend out of what would no doubt be a very large bill. "I have seamstresses I can call who would be very glad of the extra work."

"And of course you'll be well compensated for all the extra effort you're taking on our behalf."

The modiste inclined her head. The matter had been settled, and Mary would not change Amelia's mind.

She ignored the realization that she was not truly upset. In fact, she was very much looking forward to the days ahead. Edwina would make her life difficult at home, but when was that not true?

CHAPTER 5

They spent the next hour looking at dress designs and discussing fabrics. Mary was able to curtail some of the more extravagant excesses proposed by the modiste—did she really need her décolletage quite so low?—but was outvoted on many of the woman's proposals. In the end, she allowed Amelia and Madame Argent to make most of the decisions.

No mention was made of the final cost of all the gowns, which allowed her to keep her guilt at bay.

She let out a large breath when they finally left the store. "I will find a way to repay you—"

Amelia simply smiled at her. "Seeing you happy will be all the payment I demand. Well, that and I want to extract your promise to look out for me. I haven't forgotten how you saved me when that other woman was about to spill her drink all over my gown during our ball last year."

Mary let out an indelicate snort. "Alas, I am used to silent hostilities."

Amelia's smile fell. "We need to get you away from that house even if just for the season. You are more than welcome to stay with John and me. It would be wonderful to be able to spend more time together again."

Mary was tempted. "Perhaps later in the spring. I don't wish to rouse my sister's ire even further."

"I'll hold you to that. But please know that my invitation to stay with us is always open. You need only say the word."

"Lady Lowenbrock." They both turned to see a lovely woman had stopped just beside them. "It is such a pleasure to see you here."

Amelia dipped into a curtsy. "And you as well." Amelia turned to introduce her to the woman, who was named Lady Benington.

There was something about the woman's blue eyes that looked familiar, but Mary couldn't remember where they'd met. "You'll have to excuse me, but I feel as though I know you."

Lady Benington laughed. "You do indeed, although it has been quite a few years. Before I married, I was Jane Ashford. Our families were acquainted."

"Oh of course, I remember now. It must be so

nice to have Lord Ashford home from his years in the army."

Jane's eyes narrowed in speculation. "You've seen my brother recently?"

"Miss Trenton joined us for dinner yesterday with Lord Ashford and Lord Cranston. And last year the two men came up to Yorkshire to see my husband. Miss Trenton was there for a small ball we held so the neighbors could meet the new marquess. They were naturally very curious about him."

"Of course," Jane said.

Her gaze rested on Mary for several moments. Mary couldn't help but notice the small package the woman held. It was wrapped in gilt paper and reminded her of the paper that covered her brother-in-law's gifts of jewelry for Edwina.

"We were visiting the modiste. Are you here to see Madame Argent as well?"

"Oh no, I've just come from picking up something for my brother." She looked past them and smiled.

They turned to find Ashford approaching, Amelia's husband at his side. Mary saw the moment Ashford caught sight of his sister, the small hesitation in his step indicating he was thinking of turning around and making his escape. She recognized the emotion behind that small pause clearly, having experienced it more times than she could count with her own sister.

Lowenbrock's eyes lit when they settled on his

wife. "When I learned you'd gone shopping, I was hoping to find you here."

Blast his sister. How had Jane managed to appear here just when his friend was looking for his wife? He should have left the man to his own devices. The last thing he needed was to be presented with a list of young women she wanted him to court.

He'd actually considered making his excuses and escaping, but no one would ever accuse him of being a coward.

Instead, he smiled at the three women. He couldn't help but notice that Mary was, as ever, dressed demurely, but there was something about her demeanor that caught his attention.

"Have the three of you left anything behind for others to buy?" He couldn't say why, but it was Mary's reply he was most interested in hearing.

His sister handed him the package she was carrying, and he stared down at it in confusion.

"I've just been to the jeweler," she said. "He made arrangements to have Father's pocket watch repaired. As you are now the viscount, you should have it."

He could feel the muscle tensing in his jaw and forced himself to unclench it. "I think Father would have preferred Henry to have this."

Jane sighed. "Despite what you believe, Henry never desired your title."

That might be true, but it had always been clear whom their father would have preferred to be the next viscount. With a nod to his sister, he took the small, wrapped box.

Clearly hoping to ease the tension between Ashford and his sister, Amelia rushed to change the subject. "We were just getting Mary ready for the season. She'll be joining us tomorrow night at the Everly ball."

Mary raised a brow. "Perhaps. The dress might not be ready by then."

Amelia laughed. "I am sure that is your wish, but make no mistake. Madame Argent has a reputation of never disappointing a customer. She assured us the dress will be ready, so you'll have no excuse to put off your return to society."

"We'll be there as well," Jane said. "I'm sure my brother was also planning to attend."

He held back his scowl. He hadn't been planning that, but knowing his friends would also be there was inducement to go along with it. And Miss Trenton would be there to save him again from unwanted advances. "Of course, I wouldn't miss it."

His gaze must have settled on Mary for a fraction longer than what would be deemed appropriate because when he glanced at his sister again, there was an unmistakable gleam in her eye as she looked from Miss Trenton to him.

And that's when he realized what he needed to do. Once again, he would need to convince Miss Trenton to come to his rescue. Only this time she wouldn't be saving him from marriage-minded women at one ball.

The only thing that would stop his mother from parading him about town over the next few months, throwing every unmarried woman his way, would be for him to find someone with whom he didn't mind spending time.

His gaze settled on Mary Trenton again as he realized the solution to his mother and sister's matchmaking attempts was standing before him.

Miss Trenton could very well be his savior. He liked her well enough, found her intelligent and attractive. And above all, she considered him nothing more than a familial acquaintance. She hadn't shown any indication she was interested in him romantically, which made her the perfect woman to court.

He just had to find a way to speak to her in private so he could beg for her assistance. Again.

She'd have nothing to gain from the arrangement. Unless… perhaps their ruse would raise her appeal in others' eyes. Not that she would need help in that area, but men were, by their very nature, competitive. His interest in Miss Trenton could very well draw the attention of others. She could end this season betrothed. Not to him, of course, but to someone suitable. Someone worthy of her.

Did she even want to be married? It was possible she was content to continue as she was. Not everyone wed, after all. And if his parents' marriage was anything to go by, many women would be better off without an overbearing husband driving away every joy in life.

He'd have to think about how best to approach her with his proposal.

CHAPTER 6

Amelia had been correct in saying Madame Argent would have the gown ready for the ball. The dress had been delivered to Amelia's town house the morning of the event, and Mary had accepted her friend's invitation to get dressed there.

It had been a relief to escape Edwina's displeasure when she learned Mary would also be attending the Everly ball. Her sister had tried to make her feel as though she were two inches tall, going on about how she would be an embarrassment with her out-of-date clothing. But the snide smirk had been wiped clean from her face when Mary told her the Marchioness of Lowenbrock would be lending her one of her gowns.

Still, Edwina had stiffened as she glanced down at Mary's very modest bosom and told her she would look ridiculous in her friend's gown. Mary hadn't told her that Amelia had gifted her the dress and that she'd arranged for it to be altered.

The look on her sister's face when she arrived with the Lowenbrocks had been worth it.

Mary had no idea how the modiste had managed it, but the dress fit as though it had been made for her in white silk with gold trim along the edge of the bodice and a matching gold filigree pattern along the hem of the dress. It was a simple design, but the lines of the dress, the choice of fabric, and the touch of gold made it look as though it cost a great deal. She hadn't asked about the price, but for all she knew, it had.

Mary had chosen to wear the only jewelry she'd been allowed to keep after her mother's passing—a single strand of pearls at her throat paired with pearl earrings. It was simple and understated, allowing the dress to steal the show. A dress that was demure but somehow managed to hint at the curves of her figure whenever she moved.

And her hair! Amelia's maid had somehow coaxed her normally straight light brown hair to curl around her face. A light dusting of powder evened out her skin tone, and a slight hint of color tinted her lips.

For the first time in her life, Mary felt beautiful.

She sensed her sister's approach before she saw her, but with Amelia at her side, Edwina wouldn't dare to be rude.

Edwina's eyes swept over her, then swung back to

her face. Her eyes narrowed slightly when they settled on Mary's mouth, and she could almost hear what her sister was thinking.

Unseemly.

Edwina would not be happy that they'd chosen to accentuate Mary's mouth even though the color was far less obvious than the stain on Edwina's lips.

Her sister greeted Amelia, who then introduced her husband.

The new Marquess of Lowenbrock was fair-haired and handsome. If he weren't so devoted to his wife, Mary had no doubt he'd have no difficulty seducing half the women present that evening. And by the gleam in Edwina's eyes, her sister would have been one of those women.

It had never occurred to her to wonder if Edwina was faithful to her husband, but now that the thought had popped into her head, it refused to leave.

"Lady Fairbanks," he said, bowing low over her hand.

Edwina tittered, and Mary held back the urge to push her sister away. It was disturbing to see her sister behaving like a moonstruck young girl. Even more so when she was making eyes at her best friend's husband.

Amelia leaned in a little closer to Lowenbrock, who smiled down at her. "I am so pleased I was able to coax your sister into joining us this evening."

Edwina shook her head. "I am amazed at the

miracle you seem to have performed with her appearance."

"Not at all," Amelia said. "My maid merely helped Mary's natural beauty to shine."

Edwina's mouth tightened. "Indeed."

"You must excuse us," Lowenbrock cut in. "The next set is just forming, and I would like nothing more than to dance with my wife."

Edwina let out a soft sigh as she realized there would be no coaxing the man to stray.

"We will catch up later," Mary said, waving them off.

Amelia had told her that Lowenbrock was uncomfortable with attention, so she couldn't fault him for wanting to escape Edwina's embarrassing attempt to gain his notice.

She turned back to her sister, waiting for the censure she knew would come. But Edwina surprised her.

"Tell me everything you know about the marquess." Her eyes followed the couple as they took their positions on the ballroom floor.

Mary repressed her flare of annoyance. "I can tell you that Lord Lowenbrock loves his wife very much."

Edwina let out a loud breath. "That was my impression as well. Pity."

What on earth was happening? Was Edwina in the habit of conducting illicit affairs with other men?

Or was she making an exception for Lowenbrock? She knew her sister didn't love her husband, but Lord Fairbanks was a good man. He didn't deserve to be cuckolded by his wife.

"I heard he has friends who are unattached."

Mary smiled sweetly. "It is kind of you to look out for my future, but I am in London to spend time with Amelia. I am not in search of a husband."

Edwina's glare almost had her laughing out loud. Fortunately, there was a group of women standing nearby, and her sister wouldn't dare display the nastier side of her personality in such a public manner.

"I do believe at least one of his friends will be here tonight. You might remember Anthony Ashford? He's back in England now."

Edwina remained silent for several seconds. "He is the viscount now."

"Yes." Mary spotted him across the room. Their eyes met, and he bowed in greeting. "He's standing by the garden doors."

Edwina's head whipped in that direction. "How is it possible that he is even more handsome than when he was young?"

"He's not old, Edwina. He is the same age as you."

"True." The corners of her mouth turned down. "I should have waited for him."

Mary held back her retort. There was no point in

bringing up the fact that waiting would have been a waste of time since Ashford had never shown a preference for her company. "I haven't heard if Baron Cranston will be here tonight." She looked about the crowded room but was unable to spot him. He was probably dancing. She remembered how much he'd loved to dance last summer during Lowenbrock's ball.

"He's coming this way!"

Edwina's urgent whisper had her turning to face her sister. "Baron Cranston?"

"No, of course not," Edwina said with a hiss. "Ashford." Edwina turned away for a moment and tugged the neckline of her bodice down another inch. She was already in danger of falling out of her dress before the action, and Mary couldn't help but be amazed at just how far her sister was going to gain the viscount's attention.

Mary would have to be blind to miss the speculative glances that were cast his way as he moved toward them. When he finally reached her and Edwina, he bowed over Edwina's hand first before doing the same to her.

Mary couldn't hold back her amusement as she inclined her head in the direction from which he'd come. "I see that you are still breaking hearts everywhere you go."

"Everyone but yours, Miss Trenton." The twinkle in his eyes made it clear he was remembering the way she had come to his rescue the previous year. She'd danced with him and then allowed him to pay her a little too much attention, all to thwart the young women who'd hoped to become the next viscountess.

Edwina's brows drew together for a fraction of a second before her forehead smoothed out again. She placed a hand on Ashford's arm and leaned in closer. Mary held back her grimace of dismay, wondering if Edwina was going to come right out and proposition the man right in front of her.

"I'm flattered you remembered me, my lord. I was sorry to hear about your father's passing. And while you were away from the country."

"Thank you," Ashford said, taking a step back so Edwina was forced to drop her hand.

It was clear Edwina was waiting for him to say more, but when Ashford didn't, Mary changed the subject. "So whose attention are you seeking this evening? If I know the young woman in question, I'll do what I can to help you."

Her comment was only partially in jest. Mary's main goal was to make it clear to her sister that she wasn't seeking the man's attention for herself. If it wasn't for her friendship with Amelia, she doubted the viscount would even be speaking to her.

Ashford shook his head, his wince of discomfort exaggerated. "Not you as well. I can assure you that my mother and my sister have that matter well in hand."

Mary lifted one shoulder in a small shrug. "If you

change your mind, you need only ask. Speaking of your mother and sister, we should go find them. I haven't seen Lady Ashford in years."

"They're scheming over by the refreshment tables. No doubt prioritizing the list of women I should be asking to dance."

"Which is why you were on the other side of the room, standing by the garden doors."

He smiled. "Just so. But allow me to escort you to them."

Mary turned toward Edwina, expecting her to join them, but her sister's attention had been commanded by another acquaintance. An older woman who didn't seem to realize that she'd taken Edwina away from her intended prey.

"We should wait for my sister," Mary said.

Ashford lowered his voice and leaned in close. "Do you really want to? I'd rather not be the man standing next to her when her dress fails to hold her in check."

Mary couldn't hold back her snort of amusement and covered her mouth with a hand. She really should chastise the man for speaking to her in such an indelicate manner, but he was only saying what everyone else was thinking.

His grin was wicked as he held out his arm. "Shall we?"

"I would be delighted, my lord."

She didn't turn back to look at Edwina, but she could feel her sister's glare as she took his arm and allowed him to lead her away.

CHAPTER 7

Spotting Mary Trenton had made him feel like a dying man finding an oasis in the desert. Not that he'd ever experienced that himself, but he imagined it would feel very much like the relief that washed over him when he realized he had an ally in that ballroom.

As they made their way toward his family, he glanced down at the woman by his side, her hand on his arm. "Say that you'll save the waltz for me, like you did last summer."

There was an amused twinkle in her eyes when she met his gaze. "This is becoming a habit of yours. Unlike the situation at that ball, you are not the only eligible man in the room. I'm sure you can relax."

He wanted to say more, to tell her that the situation was dire. That his mother had already hinted at pairing him off with a beautiful young woman for the waltz. But while he assumed that woman was of age, she'd seemed little more than a child to him.

He could remember being eighteen, although it seemed like another lifetime, and thinking that women his age were very mature. Now, at the age of twenty-nine and after having spent far too many years in the army, they seemed almost painfully young. He couldn't imagine being forced into conversation with the young woman who'd giggled up at him and hidden behind her fan when his mother had introduced them.

"Ashford," his mother called out when they approached. "I wasn't sure we'd see you again this evening."

Somehow he refrained from rolling his eyes. They both knew his mother would have hunted him down before too much longer.

Jane's smile was far too wide. "I see you've brought Miss Trenton."

"Oh, of course," Lady Ashford said, greeting her. "It is so good to see you, my dear. It's been far too long. I was so sorry to hear about the carriage accident that took your parents' lives."

Mary looked as though she were on the verge of tears as she thanked his mother.

"I ran into Miss Trenton just yesterday on Bond Street," Jane said. "She is good friends with Lady Lowenbrock."

"It is a small world indeed," his mother said. "Ashford served with Lowenbrock."

Jane looked back in the direction from which they'd come. "Isn't that your sister? She's Lady Fairbanks now, is she not?"

Mary nodded. "Yes. Lord Fairbanks is a very generous man. He made a point of welcoming me into their house after…"

After her parents' accident.

Ashford waited for her to continue. When she didn't, he spoke into the silence. "I had the pleasure of becoming reacquainted with Miss Trenton last summer when I went up to Yorkshire to visit Lowenbrock. She was also visiting."

Unfortunately, his mother seemed intent only on her own agenda. "That is quite nice. But I am relieved you've returned Ashford, and just in time. I spotted Miss Bennett moments ago. If you hurry, you can see if she is still free for the waltz. Lady Everly assured me it would be coming soon."

He didn't even try to hide his annoyance when he saw the way Miss Trenton was looking down at her hands. His mother had all but said that she wasn't worthy of her son's attention.

"I've already asked Miss Trenton to dance the waltz with me, and she has accepted."

He met Mary's gaze, catching the way she'd glanced at his mother first. For a moment he worried that she would do something to betray the fact he hadn't spoken the truth. Yes, he'd asked her to partner with him for the waltz, but she hadn't accepted.

Thankfully, Miss Trenton came, once again, to his rescue.

"Yes," Mary said, a twinkle of amusement in her expression. "I am looking forward to it very much."

His smile widened with relief and more than a hint of genuine pleasure. Miss Mary Trenton was definitely the solution to his current situation.

Lady Fairbanks chose that moment to intrude, all but barging into their small group. She was filled with smiles and pleasantries for his family, but he caught the displeasure in her expression when she looked at Mary. He'd always found her unpleasant, even when she'd been a young girl, but had ignored her. He didn't expect the flare of anger that sparked to life within him after witnessing the slight frown Lady Fairbanks aimed at her sister. He was in no position to say—or do—anything about it, but it surprised him how much he wanted to come to Mary's rescue.

CHAPTER 8

Her relief at rejoining Amelia was vast. She hoped no one had noticed Edwina's annoyance when she'd joined Ashford's family earlier. For a moment she feared Ashford had seen Edwina's frown, but if he did, he was too polite to say anything about it.

Not that it even mattered. Everyone always forgave Edwina. As the prettier, more outgoing sister, Edwina had always enjoyed men flocking to her while Mary watched from the wings. Mary only hoped that Ashford didn't fall under Edwina's spell. Although she wouldn't be able to stop him if that happened. He was a grown man and could do whatever he wanted.

Amelia placed a hand on her arm, drawing her out of her thoughts. "Is everything all right? Perhaps I should tell John that I'm going to remain by your side tonight. What did your sister say to you when we left?"

Mary shook her head at her friend's generosity. "It was fine. Edwina won't misbehave in public." Amelia's eyes narrowed, and Mary forestalled the question. "Nor would she do anything in private beyond hurl a few insults. I don't even hear them anymore. Now tell me, are Lord Lowenbrock's sisters here? I haven't seen them yet, but with the number of people here, that isn't surprising."

Amelia shook her head. "No, not tonight. They're dining en famille at Lord Kerrick's house."

Mary winced. "I hope you didn't feel the need to attend the ball on my account."

Amelia laughed. "Much to John's dismay, I've told him that I want to experience everything this season." She leaned in close and lowered her voice. "For research."

It was a testament to how much Lowenbrock loved his wife that he'd agreed to such a thing. No one would guess that the marquess, who was charming and handsome, hated these social events. Of course, he hated even more the thought of his wife venturing out to experience them on her own.

"Speaking of whom...," Amelia said, her eyes lighting with joy as her husband approached.

Mary was surprised by the pang of remorse she felt when Lowenbrock gazed down at his wife as though she were the most important person in the world. She had no doubt that to him, she was. She wasn't jealous of Amelia—her friend deserved to be happy—and from everything she'd seen and heard, Lowenbrock was a good man. Still, she couldn't deny that a small part of her wished she could find something similar. She'd done everything to push down those youthful fantasies, but it was difficult not to believe in happily-ever-afters—and perhaps wish for one herself—when faced with the reality that they did exist.

"Ladies," Lowenbrock said with a small bow meant for the two of them before he turned to Mary. "A new set is about to start. I was hoping you would join me, Miss Trenton."

Mary glanced at Amelia, but her friend waved her forward. "Go ahead and enjoy yourself."

Mary dipped into a small curtsy. "I would be honored, my lord."

He took her arm, and together they made their way onto the ballroom floor. Mary had always enjoyed dancing and didn't care if Amelia had asked her husband to do this. After all, no one else had asked her to dance.

Well, aside from Lord Ashford, but that was only because he didn't want to be pressed into dancing with someone else.

The music started, and they began to move together through the figures of the quadrille.

"I wished to thank you," Lowenbrock said.

Mary tilted her head. "Whatever for? I'm sure there isn't a woman here who would turn down an invitation to dance with you."

Lord Lowenbrock's mouth twisted slightly and Mary laughed. "Amelia told me that you don't usually come to London for the season, but it meant a great deal to her when you accepted her invitation to join us."

Mary shook her head. "I was happy to accept. Our time in Yorkshire last year was far too short."

They fell into companionable silence after that, punctuated only with Lowenbrock's wry comments about the others present that evening. By the time the dance drew to a close, she was finding it almost impossible not to burst into riotous laughter.

He led her back to Amelia's side after that, the mischievous glint in his eyes telling her he'd been trying to elicit her mirth.

"The waltz is next," Amelia said as she took her husband's arm. "I hate to leave you here alone. Do you want to go back to your sister? Or perhaps we can seek out Lady Ashford or Lady Benington to keep you company."

Mary shook her head. "I've already accepted Lord Ashford's invitation to waltz with him, so you needn't feel guilty about abandoning me."

She wondered if Ashford realized his mother had planned that little outcome. His concern at his mother's apparent slight had been obvious from the tightening of his jaw. But he'd been looking at her, and she didn't think he'd caught the quick glance that had passed between Lady Ashford and her daughter. Their satisfaction at Ashford's declaration that he had already secured her agreement to dance with him had been unmistakable.

Lowenbrock looked over her shoulder. "Speak of the devil."

"Did I hear my name being taken in vain?"

Mary shook her head, amused despite herself. What was it about Lord Ashford that made her feel so comfortable in his presence? She'd never really known him all that well back when their families had socialized, but she felt at ease in his company.

The two men shared a look that Mary couldn't decipher before Lowenbrock whisked his wife away, telling her they should get something to drink before the next dance started.

Mary raised one brow and turned to Ashford. "What was that about?"

He lifted one shoulder. "I don't know what you mean. But I'm glad we have a few moments to speak. I wanted to apologize for forcing your hand earlier. I made it seem as though you'd already agreed, but if you've changed your mind…"

He didn't need to finish that sentence, and she couldn't deny the disappointment his words had caused. She knew, of course, that Ashford wasn't interested in her romantically, but it hurt that he was trying to back out of dancing with her.

She couldn't tell whether Ashford sensed her disappointment or if he realized his words could be taken as a rejection of her, but he gave his head a small shake and let out a harsh breath.

"I fear I've made a muddle of things. Let me begin anew. I would very much enjoy partnering with you for this next dance."

Her spirits brightened at his reassurance. "What kind of friend would I be if I abandoned you now in your hour of need?"

He smiled down at her, and her breath caught. It was a silly reaction, really, since he was just being kind. She took his arm and together they made their way to the center of the ballroom. Other couples were also taking their places. Amelia and Lowenbrock passed them, and Amelia's raised brows as she looked between her and Ashford had Mary shaking her head. Amelia would insist on making more of this waltz.

Mary would explain the situation to her friend later.

She sighed when she caught sight of Edwina, who didn't even try to hide her glare. There would be no waltz for her sister as Lord Fairbanks hated to dance. Mary had seen him chatting with some acquaintances, and then he'd disappeared. No doubt he'd quit the ballroom for the card room.

Remembering her sister's shameless flirting earlier

that evening, she couldn't help but feel a thrill of satisfaction at having bested her sister in this. How it must gall Edwina to witness her dancing with the man she'd always believed should have been hers. And a waltz, no less.

The first strains of music began, and Mary moved into his arms. All thoughts of her sister, of Amelia, of anyone else present, disappeared when she met Ashford's gaze.

CHAPTER 9

They gazed into one another's eyes, and she could almost see his thoughts as he looked down at her. For just this moment, she allowed herself to believe this was real. She wasn't given to flights of fancy. She knew a man like Viscount Ashford could have any woman he wanted, so why would he choose her?

Not that she wanted him to choose her. They were friends and nothing more.

Flustered, she looked away. What was happening to her? A man showed her a small amount of attention and already her imagination was spinning all manner of fairy-tale endings.

Ashford's voice broke into her thoughts. "I was hoping to engage your assistance with a matter that is plaguing me."

Mary took a deep breath and looked up at him. It

was almost impossible to forget that he held her so closely as they moved across the ballroom floor. They maintained a respectful distance, and his hands never wandered from their very proper positions on her upper back and hand. So why was she finding it so difficult to breathe?

"Something beyond shielding you from dancing with someone who possesses a great deal of beauty?"

She'd aimed for levity with her words, but she must have missed her mark because his eyes widened with surprise. "You must know that you've just described yourself?"

She shook her head. She knew she wasn't beautiful, but now wasn't the time for that argument. "You wanted to ask me something?"

His lips pressed together. "My mother is intent on seeing me engaged to be married by the end of the season. My sister has let me know that Mother intends to do everything in her power to see that happens. In an attempt to help, Jane has offered to assist in finding me a bride."

Mary winced. "So they've joined forces against you."

"Exactly. My mother has taken the liberty of accepting all manner of invitations on my behalf, and I fear what she'll do if I cross her. Jane has me convinced our mother would actually post a betrothal announcement to a woman of her own choosing in the newspapers. I've resigned myself to doing what I can to keep her from even thinking about something so drastic."

Her eyes widened. "Would she really do that?" She could just imagine how she would feel if her sister did the same thing to her. Fortunately, Mary was of age and couldn't be forced to wed. But while society accepted a woman breaking an engagement, a man couldn't do the same. It would call into question his honor and sully the reputation of the woman.

"I'd like to think she wouldn't, but I've been away for many years, and she's changed in that time. Become more assertive. I have no idea what she'd resort to. But I have an idea that might keep her from employing such rash measures."

When he didn't continue, she raised a brow. "You can't say all that and not tell me what it is."

He spun her, executing a swift turn that had her curls bouncing and the fabric of her gown swirling about their legs. It was impossible to miss the fact that he was very muscular. She laughed up at him, amused. His smile was crooked, one corner of his mouth lifting up. His gaze was intense, and for a moment she feared he could see through to her very soul.

"Can you not guess?"

Her thoughts in turmoil, she could only shake her head in reply. Her normal wit seemed to have scattered to the wind, cast aside when he twirled her.

"I will need to court a woman of my own choosing."

Her stomach dropped at his words, but she ignored the pang of disappointment. "Do I know this person?"

"Of course. In fact, I'm dancing with her right now."

Somehow she kept her mouth from dropping open, but she couldn't hold back the spark of pleasure his words ignited. She forced herself to speak evenly. "Surely you jest. You must know I am not angling for any such thing from you."

His brows drew together for a moment. "We'll leave aside the blow you just delivered to my ego."

His look of exaggerated wounded pride had her laughing as he executed another smooth turn.

"The safest way to make it through this season is to convince my family I am seriously considering one particular woman. You, in fact."

His words had the opposite effect on her than normal. At any other time, she'd delight in subverting the expectations of others, and it would amuse her that such a pretense would upset her sister. But for some reason, all she felt was disappointment because Ashford had just made it clear that he would never be interested in courting her. Not in earnest.

She glanced at the other waltzing couples, her gaze falling first on Amelia and her husband. It was clear to everyone that theirs was a love match. The way they looked at one another, their bodies just a fraction too close as they moved, showcased their feelings to anyone who watched.

The other couples ranged from young men and women who clearly hadn't been buffeted about by the harsh realities of the world to those poor girls who'd been paired with much older men. Some did an admirable job of hiding their displeasure at the knowledge they were destined for a practical, loveless marriage. Some didn't care. Edwina had been one of those young women, content at securing a match that would ensure she had a comfortable future. And if she only tolerated her husband's presence, at least she was one of the lucky few who had married well. Baron Fairbanks was neither young nor handsome, but at least he was a good man who put up with his wife's moods.

But Mary couldn't help feeling sorry for the young women who couldn't hide their displeasure… Or even worse, the ones who looked as though they were terrified of what their futures held. There was one young woman, clearly in her first season, who was as delicate and beautiful as a newly bloomed rose. She was waltzing with a gentleman old enough to be her grandfather, and from the look on his face as he gazed down at her, it was very likely he'd already secured her hand. Mary had to look away from the misery on the girl's face.

When she met Ashford's gaze again, the tense line

of his jaw told her he was worried she would deny him. "Are you sure you're willing to engage in such a deception, and with me? Wouldn't your family rather see you with someone younger?"

"My family likes you very much, Miss Trenton. They would be thrilled."

She let out a sigh. "I'm not in town to seek a husband. Which I suppose is a good thing since no one has shown any interest in courting me. Such a ruse wouldn't be believable."

"That's because those men are fools."

She smiled up at him, but when she saw the heat in his gaze, her thoughts scattered. She'd thought he was being polite, but there was something in his expression that caused her breath to catch. Their gazes held for what seemed like an eternity before he cleared his throat and looked away.

He swept her across the outer edge of the ballroom floor as an awkward silence settled over them. When they had completed one full circuit, he spoke again. "I understand that my proposal was unexpected, and I would be in your debt."

"Edwina would be very displeased."

"What your sister thinks doesn't matter."

"That sentiment is easy for you to say. You are not beholden to her generosity for your very livelihood."

He frowned. "You should know that you can name anything by way of repayment and it will be yours."

She looked up at him, taking in the sincerity of his expression, and found herself tempted to agree. She couldn't deny that she'd enjoy having this man pay court to her even if it was all for show.

She licked her lips and noticed the way Ashford's eyes settled on her mouth before he tore his gaze away. Which of course made her think of her earlier conversation with Amelia and her sister's criticism of her mouth.

"I will need some time to think about this."

"Of course," he said with a nod. "How much time do you need? Can I call on you tomorrow?"

She could just imagine the look on Edwina's face. "My sister won't allow us to spend time alone together so we can discuss this matter. She wouldn't want to risk your compromising me and us being forced to marry. She still wants you for herself."

Ashford shook his head. "You do know there was never anything between your sister and me? Yes, our families were neighbors and we knew one another when we were younger, but she hadn't reached the age of majority when I enlisted. And she was always too… frivolous."

Mary still remembered how Edwina had raged when Ashford enlisted.

"Besides," he continued, "that is precisely why I'm approaching you with this proposal and not someone else. You would never betray my trust by trying to trap me into compromising you."

"You place your trust too easily, my lord. We scarce know one another."

He gazed down at her, his expression serious. It was almost unsettling since she was so used to his teasing. "I trust my instincts. They've never led me astray before, and I know they won't do so now."

She took a deep breath to calm her rattled nerves. She had to remind herself that she was a practical woman who wasn't affected by Ashford's charm. She wasn't interested in him romantically. And she certainly wasn't painting scenarios of wedded bliss with him in the back of her mind.

She blamed Amelia for those thoughts, however fleeting. Her friend's very real happily-ever-after marriage was interfering with Mary's pragmatic worldview.

"You can take me for a drive in Hyde Park tomorrow."

He grinned, his normal irreverence back in place. "I look forward to it."

CHAPTER 10

He allowed himself to hope the future wouldn't be quite as dire as he'd feared. Mary Trenton was going to come to his rescue—again. He'd be able to stay in town for the rest of the season, spending time with the friends he hadn't seen over the past winter. Best of all, he wouldn't be forced into a union he didn't want.

The following afternoon, he made his way to Baron Fairbank's town house. The day was overcast, but thankfully it didn't look like it would rain. He needed to speak to Miss Trenton in private and settle this matter once and for all.

A stern-faced butler opened the door and showed him into the drawing room. He'd told the man he was there to see Miss Trenton, but instead, the baroness swept into the room minutes later.

"My lord," she said with a deep curtsy. "I wasn't

expecting you to call. I've made plans to visit a friend, but I can send word that those plans have changed."

The way she stood just a little too close set his nerves on edge. The flagrant attention made him more than a little uncomfortable. Especially since he'd shown preference for the woman's sister. But given everything Mary had told him about Edwina's former interest in him, he wasn't surprised.

Still, he needed to nip this unwelcome attention in the bud. Determined to keep a tight rein on his annoyance, he dipped his head in a formal bow. "There is no need to go out of your way on my behalf. I invited Miss Trenton to ride with me this afternoon."

Lady Fairbanks frowned. "I'm not sure that will be wise. We wouldn't want to cause a scandal."

"We'll be at Hyde Park along with at least half of London society. We'll be in view at all times."

She dropped onto the settee, but Ashford remained on his feet. It might be rude, but he wanted to make sure the baroness knew she needed to abandon whatever misconceptions she still held about the nature of their relationship.

"She didn't tell me about this." Her brows drew together as she searched for a reason to forbid their outing.

For a moment he feared she'd locked Mary in her chamber. He relaxed when he heard the sound of light footsteps coming down the hallway.

Mary stepped into the room a moment later, and he drank in the sight of her. She was modestly dressed in a sky-blue gown, a wrap around her shoulders. He greeted her with a warm smile.

"It is a pleasure to see you this afternoon, my lord."

He caught the twinkle in her eyes before she dipped her head and curtsied.

He approached and took her hand, bowing over it. "The pleasure is all mine, Miss Trenton."

They both wore gloves, so there was nothing scandalous about the action, but the slight hiss from Lady Fairbanks was unmistakable. Mary's eyes met his, and from the amusement he could see within her gaze, it was clear she was enjoying tormenting her sister.

Before Lady Fairbanks could do something as brash as suggest she join them—a request he would be forced to refuse—he turned to face her again. "Please don't allow us to keep you."

Her lips pressed together in a firm line before she rose to her feet again. "I'll call for my sister's maid to accompany you."

"There would be nowhere for her to sit as I've brought my phaeton. It only has room for two." Lady Fairbanks opened her mouth to protest, but he continued. "As you no doubt know, it is completely open. I promise that nothing untoward will happen to your sister." Even if he had such designs, there would be no way to keep from having their every movement observed.

Lady Fairbanks looked like she wanted to protest further and he waited. Finally she nodded. "Of course, my lord. Our families have been close for as long as I can remember. I am sure Mary couldn't be in safer hands."

He turned back to Miss Trenton and was surprised to see her smile had dimmed somewhat. He vowed to do everything in his power to bring it back.

He moved to her side. "Shall we?"

She nodded up at him and took his arm.

"It was a pleasure seeing you again, Lady Fairbanks. Please give my regards to your husband."

Her expression tightened at his casual dismissal. Good.

They made their way from the house, but once the door closed behind her, Mary froze in pace. "What on earth is that?"

She was staring at his carriage, her eyes wide.

Somehow he held back a laugh. "My phaeton."

She took a step closer, her head tilted to one side as she looked over the vehicle, finally settling on the high seat. "I've never actually seen one that was quite so tall. I can see why they have a reputation for being unsafe."

"I'll admit it was an indulgence, but I couldn't resist having one."

Her eyes remained on the seat. "How on earth am

I going to get up there? And more importantly, how do I keep from falling off?"

A quick glance back at the house showed him that Lady Fairbanks was watching them from the drawing room window.

"Come now," he said. "I never took you for a coward." He leaned closer and lowered his voice even though there was no chance they'd be overheard. "Your sister is watching us right now."

As he knew they would, his words caused her to straighten her spine. "I am not afraid, just prudent. But if you can ride in that thing, so can I."

"That's the spirit. And never fear, I brought something to help you get in."

He reached into the passenger side of the vehicle and pulled out the small set of stairs he'd placed there himself. He positioned it next to the phaeton and held out a hand.

Mary smiled at him as she placed her hand in his. She gripped it tightly as she climbed up the four steps, wavering slightly on the top one before taking a deep breath and placing her foot on the little ledge at the side of the carriage. He moved closer and placed a hand at her waist to keep her steady.

She didn't loosen her grip even after she was seated.

"This was a bad idea," he said. "We can try again tomorrow with another carriage—"

"And have Edwina think me a coward? Never. But you must promise not to drive too fast."

"You have my word." He squeezed her hand in reassurance.

With a deep breath, she released her grip and placed her hands in her lap.

He left the small set of steps next to the town house door since there was nowhere to stow it on the carriage. The butler would probably have a footman bring it around to the side of the house, but he didn't really care if it went missing. He only needed it for today. It wasn't as though he was planning to take another woman out for such a public ride.

Although perhaps he'd need it again for Mary. They might have to go to Hyde Park regularly.

He sprang up into the carriage and took the ribbons into his hands. He couldn't hold back his grin when Mary shook her head at the ease with which he'd completed the task.

At his soft command, the matched pair of grays began to move and he turned the carriage toward Hyde Park. He loved driving his phaeton and normally was content to ride in silence, but today he wanted to get straight to the point. He didn't want to press the matter though, so instead he commented on the weather.

She let out a sigh. "We both know why we're here, and it's not to comment on the fact we can see a sliver of blue through the clouds this afternoon." Her tone wasn't promising.

"In my defense, it *is* a pleasant day."

The look she gave him was a mixture of exasperation and amusement. It gave him a small amount of hope as to how this conversation would end.

"What you propose would put me in a very awkward position."

He glanced at her, but her expression was carefully neutral. "How so?"

"Edwina was already displeased with me after the ball last night, and again this morning when your flowers arrived. After our performance this afternoon, she'll be unbearable."

His grip tightened on the ribbons, and he had to force his fingers to relax lest he cause the horses to rear back. He had to take a deep breath before asking the next question. "She wouldn't hurt you, would she?"

The look of horror on Mary's face did much to ease the tightness in his chest.

"Good heavens, no. But I am dependent on her. She can do much to make my life miserable without causing me physical harm."

As they reached their destination, the carriage slowed and they joined the line of vehicles making their way into Hyde Park. Ashford had heard the crowds could be suffocating during the fashionable hour, but he'd thought that an exaggeration. It wasn't.

Their conversation halted for some time as he nodded in greeting to several groups of people who'd gathered near the park's entrance. No doubt they wanted to take an inventory of everyone there that afternoon.

When Mary smiled and waved at almost everyone they passed, he leaned toward her. "Do you know who all these people are?"

She lifted one shoulder in a small shrug. "I know a few of them. But I'm sure they know who we are. No doubt word of our outing today is already spreading from person to person."

"Then you should pretend to be vastly amused by what I am saying to you right now."

"Oh, I'm definitely amused by the spectacle we seem to be creating. It doesn't hurt that we're so high up and everyone can see us. I feel as though I'm on a stage."

He laughed before turning his attention back to the road. His sister had warned him that he shouldn't make an appearance here with a young woman unless he was serious about pursuing her. Jane had shown, yet again, that she knew London society better than he. Which meant he really needed to listen to her advice.

But he most definitely wouldn't tell her his courtship of Mary Trenton was a ruse since he couldn't be sure what she'd do with that information. It was possible she'd sympathize and help him, but too many years had passed since they'd grown up together. And when they were children, she'd always seemed to delight in doing the opposite of what she should. No, it was better to keep Jane in the dark about his true motivation for today's outing. He had no doubt she'd hear about it soon enough.

"I'm beginning to think this wasn't a good idea," Mary said as she waved to yet another small group of people.

She caught her lower lip between her teeth, and he realized she had a nice mouth. Plump lips, ripe for kissing. He tore his gaze away from her, forcing himself to concentrate on driving. His horses weren't used to going so slowly, and it wouldn't do to cause an accident because he was paying too much attention to Miss Trenton's mouth.

"Does that mean you've decided not to help me?" He told himself the reason for his disappointment wasn't because he'd been looking forward to seeing more of the beautiful woman seated next to him.

She was biting that lower lip again, and he had to fight back a groan. "I'd been leaning toward saying yes."

His spirits soared at her words, but it was obvious she still wasn't sure.

"Is there anything I can say or do that can help to sway you to my cause?"

"Well, I will admit that I'm enjoying the attention we're causing more than I should."

That distracting mouth turned up in an unrepentant grin. He forced his gaze to remain on hers.

"At the very least this will be a nice test as to how quickly gossip spreads among the ton. I wonder how long it will take my mother or my sister to hear we were seen together at Hyde Park."

"I'd say Lady Benington already knows. She's coming toward us now."

His gaze swung forward as he scanned the other carriages and the people milling about on foot, searching for his sister. The peal of Mary's laughter told him she'd gotten one over on him.

"You're going to have to do much better than that, my lord, if we're to keep up this ruse. You look like a little boy who's been caught sneaking into the kitchens for a treat when you should be in bed."

No, he absolutely would not allow his thoughts to swing toward the bedroom. "At any rate, I'm sure it won't take long before word of our outing reaches her ears." He nodded at one of the men whose name he couldn't remember. "I'll admit I'm a little taken aback by how crowded it is here. I was told this was the place to be seen, but I had no idea everyone in London would also be here."

Mary let out a soft sigh. "Yes, I still remember the chaos when we were in London for Edwina's season."

"And during your season?"

"I didn't have one. My parents had passed away at

that point, and I was already living with my sister and her husband."

"And they couldn't be bothered bringing you to town?" He couldn't ignore the anger that thought caused him. He'd made it a point to discover everything he could about Lord Fairbanks. The man never missed a session of the House of Lords, so there would have been no excuse to deprive her of a season.

"Oh no, it wasn't like that at all. Lord Fairbanks wanted me to join them, but I couldn't stomach the idea of being shepherded around town by my sister."

He started to frown but then remembered they were on display. He didn't want anyone to think he found anything unpleasant about being with Miss Trenton. "Are you saying she wouldn't have done it?"

Mary lifted one shoulder. "She would have had to. But…" She gave her head a shake. "Never mind—it isn't really my place to share details about her personal life."

"But they affect you."

"Not really, no. We'll just say that she can be insufferable. When spring comes around every year and they leave for London, I look forward to having the time to myself. You have siblings, so I'm sure you understand."

He did. But now that he'd come into the title and was back in England, he could do whatever he wanted. Well, most of the time anyway. His mother's arrival in town and her insistence on seeing him wed was an unwelcome complication.

"At any rate, that is enough about me. Tell me, my lord, why I should indulge you in this ridiculous scheme of yours."

CHAPTER 11

He wanted to press her for more details about her living situation, but it wasn't his place to do so. They were on friendly terms, yes, but they weren't *friends*, per se.

"Because you have a good heart and don't wish to see me forced into a marriage not of my own choosing?"

Mary let out an indelicate snort, then raised a hand to cover her mouth. He couldn't hold back his own huff of amusement.

Mary dropped her hand and sighed. "As I've said, Edwina will be most displeased. She had her heart set on becoming your viscountess and ranted for some time when you enlisted."

He frowned. Mary had mentioned that to him when they'd met again last summer at Lowenbrock's estate. Their families lived close to one another and had often attended the same local events. He'd been a youth himself at the time and spent most of the year away at school. He still found it difficult to believe that Mary's sister had been scheming to trap him into marriage before she'd even come out in society. Did all women spend their youth dreaming of their upcoming marriages?

"She's married to Baron Fairbanks now, so what I do and who I choose to court has nothing to do with her."

Mary tilted her head to one side and examined him. "She'll want to murder me when I get home later. No doubt she'll insist I dissuade you from courting me."

A twinge of guilt pierced him at the difficult situation he was causing this woman. "Will it be that bad?"

"Bad enough, but as long as we are in town, she'll behave. She won't want Amelia to think she's mistreating me."

Which meant that wouldn't be the case after the season was over. "I shouldn't have asked you to do this. It is too much."

Mary waved one hand. "On the contrary, this was precisely the push I needed to make changes in my life."

A hint of alarm went through him. "In what way?"

"Father settled a small amount on me. I don't know if it's enough to live on, but I intend to make inquiries about moving into a small home of my own. I was too afraid to do so before now. Nervous about starting out alone, somewhere where I didn't know anyone. But perhaps Amelia and her husband can help me. I'm afraid I'm at a loss as to how to proceed."

"Let me help you." The words were out of his mouth before he realized he'd intended to make the offer, but he wouldn't take them back. Not just because he wanted to pay this woman back for helping him but because the very thought of Mary Trenton setting out on her own unsettled him.

"I'm sure Lord Lowenbrock wouldn't mind, especially if Amelia asked him. He would do anything for her. And he wouldn't need to go out of his way. I'm sure he could ask his solicitor—"

"*I* will help you, Miss Trenton. I insist. It is the very least I can do since my scheme is responsible for upsetting your entire life." He winced at the truth of his words. She was behaving selflessly on his behalf, and it was his duty to help her.

Mary looked away, and they drove in silence for almost a full minute. Finally he couldn't bear it any longer. "Please tell me what you're thinking. If you're reconsidering, I'll understand." He'd also be disappointed, but he wouldn't tell her that.

She wet her lips with her tongue, and he found his eyes glued to the small movement. He hadn't even realized she was looking at him again. He glanced away for a moment to gather his composure before meeting her gaze.

"What did you have in mind, my lord?"

There was an odd quality to her voice. Her shoulders were stiff and her voice sharper than it had been during their entire conversation. He wondered why that would be.

"I have several estates, and many have smaller houses attached to them. I'm sure we could find something that would suit you."

"And the rent for those houses?"

He lifted one shoulder in a casual shrug. "Given the way I'm upending your life with my request, I wouldn't expect you to pay me rent."

She sucked in a sharp breath, causing his confusion to ratchet up another notch.

"Did I say something wrong?"

"I'm going to be direct with you, although what I need to say is something that makes me more than a little uncomfortable."

Her nose scrunched up, and he had a difficult time concentrating on the task of driving. He couldn't imagine why she was so upset.

"I would expect no less from you."

She straightened her shoulders and looked him directly in the eye. "Are you asking me to be your mistress?"

His thoughts scattered at her question. "What? Why…?" He closed his mouth and took a deep breath. He winced when he saw that an acquaintance was waving him over to where he and his wife were standing next to a park bench. But this wasn't a conversation he could leave hanging, and so he gave the man a small shrug as the carriage passed him.

He could feel Miss Trenton's eyes boring into him. "No, of course not. I would never disrespect you in such a way."

Mary let out a small huff of laughter, shaking her head as though unable to believe she'd actually asked him that question.

"Why would you assume that?"

The corners of her mouth turned down in a small grimace. "You can blame Amelia for that. She led me to believe that I would need to watch out for men who would make such a proposition."

"And when I offered to set you up on one of my properties..." He shook his head. "I can see why you needed to ask, but my proposal was genuine and without any such conditions. You're doing me the greatest of favors and putting your own future in a state of uncertainty as a result. It is the very least I can do to ensure you don't suffer any ill outcome as a result."

Mary's eyes roamed over his face and he held her gaze, hoping she could see he was being genuine.

Finally, with a sigh, she smiled at him. "I accept your offer, my lord. And I must say that it will be entertaining to watch my sister tie herself up in knots this season."

He could only shake his head. "I can't say that I understand her obsession with me."

"I wouldn't call it an obsession. You represent a disappointment to her. She'd built up all manner of fairy tales in her head about you sweeping her off her feet and falling head over heels in love with her. When you enlisted instead, those dreams died."

"I had the impression Lord Fairbanks was a good man. I hope he doesn't mistreat her… or you, for that matter."

"Oh no, he's very kind. And he puts up with her ever-changing moods with greater patience than other men would. But he's older and marrying him wasn't quite the fairy tale she'd envisioned for herself."

He had no answer for that, and so he let the subject of Lady Fairbanks drop. "I can't even begin to thank you for your assistance in this matter."

Mary smiled. "It's no hardship, my lord. Besides, it will save me from sitting on the outer edges at all the entertainments to which Amelia intends to drag me."

He frowned. "Why would you sit on the side?"

She huffed out a small laugh. "I'm not young nor am I pretty. And despite the fact that I'm not looking for a husband, I wasn't looking forward to being ignored while girls much younger than me had their pick of all the men looking for brides."

He stared at her, certain at first that she was jesting. But after several moments he realized that wasn't the case. "I can assure you, Miss Trenton, that no one would pass you over."

She shook her head, her light brown curls dancing about her face with the vigorous movement. "You needn't flatter me. I've already agreed to help you."

He could only wonder at why she would think herself unworthy of attention. It struck him then that if he was truly in search of a wife, she would be at the very top of that list.

Who was he trying to deceive—she would comprise the entire list. Still, he couldn't help but wonder if her sister's criticisms were at the root of Mary's insecurities.

"This isn't empty flattery. Any man would be fortunate to have you." He winced slightly at his choice of words. "As a wife, that is."

Mary's mouth lifted at the corners, and he couldn't help but wonder if she was laughing at him. "As you say, my lord."

CHAPTER 12

The following morning, Mary headed down to the breakfast room early, hoping to avoid her sister. Edwina had been out for the evening when Ashford dropped her off the previous day after their carriage ride, and she'd been able to avoid her sister for the rest of the night. Edwina hadn't invited her to the rout she was attending, and Mary hadn't asked to go along with her and Lord Fairbanks. Amelia wasn't going to be there, so there was no point in tagging along and subjecting herself to her sister's glares.

But despite returning long after Mary was already asleep, her sister was already up and was waiting for her in the breakfast room. It was unheard of for Edwina to be up so early. Unfortunately, Lord Fairbanks wasn't present, so she couldn't count on his presence to shield her.

With a forced smile, she wished her sister good morning and settled into a seat at the table. She reached for a serving of toast but ignored the eggs. She knew this conversation was going to be unpleasant and wanted to get out of the room as soon as possible.

Edwina said nothing as she poured her tea, which only caused Mary's nerves to stretch further. The sooner Edwina berated her, the sooner she could move past it and on with the rest of her day. Maybe she could call on Amelia this morning. She'd been meaning to visit the lending library with her friend, and today seemed as good a day as any.

"Lord Fairbanks and I have come to a decision."

Mary tensed. "About what?"

Edwina took a sip of her tea and smiled at her. Mary knew that smile. It meant that her sister thought she'd won. Perhaps she had convinced her husband to send her back to their country estate.

"Yes. We have decided that it is time for you to wed. And no, it won't be to Lord Ashford." Edwina's mouth twisted on the man's name. "I'm sure we can find a match that's much more suitable for your prospects."

The smirk on her sister's face had ice flowing through Mary's veins. She'd known her sister would be unhappy about Mary's name being linked to Ashford's, but she'd never imagined Edwina would try to force her to wed someone of her choosing.

Mary was glad now that she'd taken that first step toward freedom. She'd held back for far too long, nervous about the prospect of being on her own. But she had friends who would help her get settled. She'd imagined it would be Amelia who'd come to her rescue. And while she'd hated the idea of asking for such a favor, she'd known her friend would help her to set her plan in motion.

She never imagined that Lord Ashford would be the one to insist on helping her. But he was right. This pretend courtship had barely started and already it had turned her entire world upside down.

"I shall give this matter careful consideration," Mary said, hoping her sister would let the subject drop.

She wasn't surprised at the too-sweet smile that spread across Edwina's face. "I've already given the matter much thought. I know that Lord Gravenhurst is searching for a wife. We'll have to make a point of seeking him out later tonight."

It took everything in her power not to frown. Lord Gravenhurst was ancient and had already buried two wives.

"Well, I'll leave you to your breakfast now."

Mary watched as her sister stood and swept from the room. She was aware of the footman who stood by the door and so she continued with her breakfast. She didn't need the servants gossiping about her. Edwina would love to have proof that her declaration had caused Mary distress and would grill her maid about Mary's demeanor during breakfast.

She finished her toast and her tea, her thoughts in turmoil the entire time. When she finally pushed away from the table, she already had her plan in place.

Mary was of age, and so Edwina couldn't force her to wed. Still, her sister could make her life a living hell. The last thing Mary wanted was to sit through the throng of older men her sister was about to parade before her. No, it was time to begin taking her steps toward a life of freedom.

She made her way up to her bedroom and wrote a quick note to Amelia. Her sister would read it, of course, and so she kept it brief.

I am very happy to accept your invitation.

I look forward to seeing you this afternoon.

—M. Trenton

Amelia had invited her to move in with her and her husband while they were in town for the season, but Mary had assured her that wouldn't be necessary. She'd vastly underestimated her sister's displeasure when she learned Lord Ashford was courting her.

She handed the note to a maid and then settled in to wait. She wanted to start packing but couldn't risk alerting her sister to her plans. It was entirely possible that Edwina would have her bundled up and sent back to their country estate if she learned Mary was about to escape.

One hour passed, and Mary began to question the wisdom of sending the note. It was entirely possible that Edwina had torn it up. But would she do that when she very much wanted to count the wife of a marquess among her personal acquaintances? Surely she wouldn't risk doing something to jeopardize that connection.

Mary was beginning to think she should set out herself instead of sitting there, waiting. If she was going to begin a new life of independence soon, she needed to start taking action herself instead of waiting for others.

Her decision made, she stood and crossed the room. Her hand was on the doorknob when a knock caused her to start. Bracing herself for another uncomfortable interaction with her sister, Mary opened the door. Her tension fled when she found it was a footman.

He gave her a small bow. "You have a caller, Miss Trenton."

Would Amelia be here already? Perhaps it was Lord Ashford. "Who is it?"

"Lady Lowenbrock. She is in the drawing room with your sister."

Relief flooded through her. "Thank you," she said, pulling her bedroom door closed behind her.

He stepped aside, and she made her way downstairs. It didn't even bother her that she was leaving with nothing. Her sister wouldn't dare hold back her belongings. Not with Amelia there to witness their exchange.

Her new life was beginning today. She should have left her sister's household years ago. Despite the bravado she'd shown the world and her practical nature, the thought of being on her own had frightened her. Even though she and Edwina weren't on the best of terms, at least they were family. But after this morning's conversation, it was clear that their relationship would never recover. Better to strike out on her own than to be forced into marrying someone and giving him control over her life and her person.

How ironic that she and Lord Ashford found themselves in a similar position.

She didn't hesitate as she entered the drawing room. Edwina was going on about having Amelia and Lowenbrock over for dinner one day so they could become better acquainted. Amelia murmured something about hoping she could fit it into their engagements. Her words were polite but distant. When her eyes settled on Mary, however, her entire face lit up. She rose and they embraced.

Mary couldn't resist glancing at her sister over her friend's shoulder. Edwina's smile was still in place, but her face looked as though it were a frozen mask.

Amelia turned back to her sister. "I am so happy that Mary has indulged my request to spend time with me over the next few weeks."

Edwina's smile faltered. "You're already spending time together."

Amelia turned to Mary and grabbed her hand. "Yes, but she's finally agreed to come stay with us for a little while. We see so little of one another, and I find that I've become greedy for her company."

Edwina's expression hardened, and Mary saw the moment she realized her sister's seemingly innocent note—which she'd no doubt read before allowing it to be delivered to the marchioness—was the reason Mary was about to escape her household. As well as her plans for Mary's future.

"We wouldn't want to put you out—"

"Oh, it's no inconvenience at all. I thought I would be content to have Mary join me in town for the season, but I've been longing for even more of her company." Edwina opened her mouth to interrupt but Amelia continued. "I've never had a sister. It's always been just me. I know you'll miss her, but you must allow me to indulge this desire."

Edwina stood, the corners of her mouth lifting in a patently false smile. "Of course. And that will give me a reason to visit."

Mary inclined her head. "I'm sure it will feel as though I never moved out."

Given that she and Edwina rarely spent any time together, she sincerely hoped that proved to be true. The last thing she wanted was to endure endless calls while her sister pretended to be a doting sibling.

Edwina turned to her. "Have you already asked the staff to pack your belongings? How long will you be gone—one week?"

Amelia saved her once again. "I know you'll miss your sister terribly, but I was hoping Mary could spend the rest of the season with me. I can have one of my maids come and help with the packing."

"Oh no, that won't be necessary. It will be no problem to arrange for my sister's belongings to be delivered to your town house."

Amelia let go of Mary's hand and approached Edwina. "I'm so glad to hear that. You have no idea how happy I am right now. I am in your debt."

And those were the magic words that turned Edwina's stiff smile into a genuine one. Ever the social climber, her sister was already plotting all manner of ways to turn this situation to her advantage.

"We'll miss you here," Edwina said.

For one horrible moment, Mary thought her sister was going to hug her. Visions of Edwina trying to squeeze the life out of her flitted through Mary's mind.

Whether or not Amelia sensed the tension, she broke the awkward moment. "I'll be sure to send a footman in a few hours to collect Mary's belongings. I'm already asking so much from you in sacrificing the company of your sister, so please allow me to do this."

Edwina inclined her head in agreement. When

she met Mary's eyes again, what Mary saw there sent shivers down her spine. Her sister was more than just angry… she was livid. Mary had outmaneuvered her in arranging her escape. Now that Mary wasn't relying on her and Lord Fairbanks, Edwina couldn't force her to wed someone of her own choosing.

If Mary had even the smallest hope of returning to live with her sister in the country, that hope evaporated after seeing the glint of anger in her sister's eyes.

"I won't keep you any longer today." Amelia twined her arm through Mary's and began to lead her from the drawing room. "I am so glad you've indulged me in this."

They accepted their hats and cloaks from the butler. Mary didn't turn around as they made their way from the town house. This would be the last time she'd reside with her sister. There would be no going back after today. She'd wondered if even a small part of her would feel some kind of remorse when she finally broke away, but she only felt relief.

Amelia kept up a steady stream of chatter until the carriage door closed behind them. The silence that followed was almost deafening.

When the carriage began to move, Mary grabbed one of Amelia's hands and gave it a firm squeeze. "I am in your debt. I feared that my note might have been too obscure."

"I was so worried when I received it. I never

expected you to take me up on my offer. What happened?"

Mary's mouth twisted for a moment. "She threatened to marry me off to someone of her choosing. Which means…"

"Old but wealthy."

"Exactly. Someone she can brag about being connected to but with whom I would never be happy."

Amelia shook her head. "I know it's a common practice, but how could she do that to you?"

Mary raised a brow. "I daresay that describes the relationships of most of the ton. Which means that for every love match, like yours, countless others must enter into practical unions that suit their families more than themselves."

Amelia let out a small huff of air. "Well, you are not going to be one of those people."

Mary gazed out the window, trying not to think too much about the future. Would she be lonely in her new life? It was one thing to be alone when her sister went into town for the spring. That was a finite amount of time. Mary scarcely had enough time for the daily tension of her normal life to leave before her sister was sweeping back with stories of all the things she'd done and what everyone else was doing. And at least the gossip meant Edwina wasn't fixing her critical gaze on her sister.

Mary had never been alone for longer than a few

months. Her future now stretched out before her, years where she would be on her own. But given the alternative, she had no regrets. She could do whatever she wanted during the next few months before heading out to her quiet life in the country.

"Lord Ashford is going to find me somewhere to stay. He assures me that his family's holdings are vast and that he's certain he can find something appropriate." Amelia's mouth had dropped open. "I know you said that your husband would find me a cottage where I can live a life of quiet contemplation, but…" She lifted one shoulder, stopping herself from revealing the truth about her agreement with Ashford.

"We can't allow that," Amelia said after several seconds had passed. Her voice dropped into a whisper. "Everyone will assume you are his mistress."

Mary couldn't hold back her giggle at the ridiculous statement. "No one will care, Amelia. Who would even know where I went after the season was over?"

"Your sister—"

"Won't say a word if she thinks it might reflect poorly on her."

Amelia didn't say anything, but there was something in the way her friend was looking at her that told Mary she very much wanted to. She let out a sigh. "You needn't fear—Ashford hasn't asked me to be his mistress."

"But he's setting you up in a house."

"He knows my family… It's charity. I mentioned something about you and Lowenbrock helping me to find somewhere to live, and he offered to help."

Amelia crossed her arms. "And you took his help over ours?"

"His estate isn't all the way up in Yorkshire. I love you, Amelia, but I'm not sure I'm ready to move that far away."

Amelia huffed out a snort of amusement, bumping her shoulder against Mary's. "You're terrible. Now tell me everything about what is happening between you and Ashford. I'm beginning to think you won't need that *charity* by the time the season comes to an end."

Somehow she held back a wince. She hated lying to her closest friend, but she and Ashford had agreed that they needed to keep their agreement a secret for now.

"I don't know what you mean."

Amelia scowled. "Don't be coy with me. I know the two of you were seen together at Hyde Park yesterday."

"How on earth did you hear about that?" The question was out before she realized just how silly it was. Of course Amelia had heard about their outing. Mary had seen the stares and whispering and imagined speculation was running rampant about the two of them. That would only get worse as the season progressed and Ashford continued to make her the focus of his attention.

"Why didn't you tell me? Lord Cranston told John and he, of course, told me. Apparently everyone is talking about it."

This time she did wince. This was the outcome they'd hoped for, but it was more than a little unsettling to know she was the focus of so much gossip. She who'd never had any attention paid to her. It was no wonder Edwina was so angry.

"It was only one carriage ride."

"Through Hyde Park during the fashionable hour when everyone was there to see you."

Mary tilted her head. "I don't recall seeing you there."

Amelia let out a breath, her annoyance clear. "That's as good as declaring his intentions toward you. So I'm asking you again, what is going on between the two of you?"

"Lord Ashford and I are friends." Which wasn't a lie. It just wasn't the complete truth about why they would soon be spending so much time together. "I can say with absolute certainty that Ashford does not have any romantic intentions toward me."

Amelia slumped back against the cushions of the carriage bench. "That doesn't mean things can't change. We'll just have to make him see what a catch you are." She glanced sideways at her, a grin forming. "It won't take too much effort really. He already likes you, and you're very attractive. We just need to change the way he sees you. Help him realize the two of you could be more than friends."

Mary couldn't hold back the yearning at her friend's statement. But she couldn't imagine any man looking at her the way Lowenbrock looked at Amelia. Nor the way the man's brothers-in-law looked at their wives. Ashford would never see her as more than an accomplice in keeping him safe from the marriage mart.

Still, it would be fun to pretend. She hated the idea of deceiving Amelia, but if she was being completely honest with herself, she was looking forward to the months ahead. It would be the closest Mary would ever come to the real experience of being courted.

She wasn't certain she could act the part of lovesick fool, but she'd do her best to make everyone believe she was coming to care for him. It shouldn't be too difficult since she already enjoyed his company.

And heaven knew the man was handsome. With his wide shoulders, blue eyes, and attractive features, would she even need to act? Amelia already believed there was something more than friendship between the two of them.

It was too bad Mary knew it was all pretend. She would have enjoyed having him court her in earnest even if nothing came of it in the end.

CHAPTER 13

They didn't go out that first night, something for which Mary was grateful. The last thing she needed was to run into her sister. It would happen soon, but she needed a little time to brace herself for their future meetings.

Edwina sent over her trunks, and her dresses had already been sent from the modiste to Amelia's house. Amelia must have already informed Madame Argent about her change in address.

Lord Ashford didn't call that first day, but he did the next. Along with a good number of guests for an afternoon tea party Amelia had already planned.

"I don't think fear of seeing your sister should keep you at home," her friend had said. "But for today we can have society come to us."

And come they did. A revolving door of guests

who took some light refreshments and mingled, then left to prepare for their evening entertainments.

Through it all, Ashford was a constant, steady presence. He seemed to know every man who came through the town house doors—or at least he acted as though he did. She was finding it next to impossible to remember people's names five minutes after they'd been introduced. She blamed her scattered thoughts on the way her life had been completely upended.

She couldn't blame Ashford for that fact. She'd agreed to his scheme knowing that Edwina would be upset. She'd never imagined her sister would actually try to force her to wed a man of her choosing, but now that she'd had some time to get over the shock, she realized she'd been naive. Edwina was never going to allow Mary to live with her and Lord Fairbanks forever.

She tried to distract herself, going out of her way to speak to all of the guests. But she couldn't forget her sister's criticisms, especially when she realized that Ashford's gaze kept dropping to her mouth. He kept hovering around her, and she wondered if he was being so attentive because he felt responsible for her current circumstances. Her nerves were stretched taut, and finally she couldn't hold back the question when she caught him looking at her mouth yet again.

"Why would my sister say my mouth is unseemly?"

Ashford's eyes rose to meet hers, and within them she caught a flash of something she couldn't identify. He almost looked guilty, as though she had caught him doing—or thinking—something he shouldn't be.

"I apologize—"

"No," she said, holding up a hand. She resisted the urge to grab the man by the shoulders and shake him. "I don't want an apology; I want an answer to my question."

Ashford closed his eyes for a moment. When he opened them again, he gave a curt nod. "All right, I'll tell you, but not here. This isn't the type of conversation one has in polite company."

A zing of something Mary could only guess was anticipation surged through her. Finally she was going to get an answer to a question that had always puzzled her. She gave a nod of acceptance.

Their eyes met and held for several long moments. There was heat in Ashford's gaze, and she couldn't help but wonder if he felt the same sense of anticipation that she did.

"We'll talk about this later." There was a husky quality to his voice that caused a riot of sensation within her. When Ashford turned to leave, she realized he was going to put her off.

"My lord." Her voice was loud enough now for others to hear.

He turned to face her again, one brow raised in

question. When his eyes narrowed, she realized he was afraid she was going to ask her question to the room at large. But even she wasn't brave enough for that.

"Lady Lowenbrock mentioned that her sister-in-law plans to make changes to the garden here as a gift to her brother."

"I heard something about that. Apparently Lady Kerrick has become sought after for her skills in the area, even more so since she rarely accepts requests for her services."

Mary nodded. "Exactly. I thought that perhaps we could ask Lord and Lady Lowenbrock to give us a tour of the gardens as they stand now. Then we'll be in a better position to appreciate the improvements when they're complete."

His mouth firmed briefly before he nodded. Which told her everything she needed to know—that he'd hoped to avoid having this discussion with her altogether.

She pressed her advantage. "Give me just one moment to ask them if now would be a good time for the tour."

His gaze settled on her, sending heat through her. "I am, as ever, at your service."

Good heavens, he'd certainly come around quickly. She returned his smile, but as she turned to walk away, she realized he'd somehow gained the upper hand in their exchange. She might have surprised him with her unexpected question and her insistence that they have this conversation now, but he'd recovered quickly.

When she reached Amelia's side, she pulled her friend aside and asked if she and her husband could escort her and Ashford through the gardens.

"I would like nothing better," Amelia said. She lowered her voice before adding, "I know you're planning something."

Mary sighed. "I need to speak to Ashford alone. Perhaps you and Lowenbrock could allow us to fall back for a little bit on our walk."

Amelia's gaze roamed over her face. But if there was one thing living under her sister's ever-present gaze had taught her, it was to keep her emotions hidden.

Amelia must have realized she would get no further information until Mary was ready. With a sigh she went to fetch her husband, and Mary returned to Ashford's side.

"What did you tell her?" Ashford asked.

Mary lifted one shoulder in a shrug. "Only that we needed to have a discussion and that a tour of the gardens would give us that opportunity."

"And what if others wish to join us on this tour?"

Mary's mouth opened, then snapped closed again. The idea hadn't occurred to her.

He let out a small chuckle and held out his arm for her to take. When she slipped her hand into his elbow, he leaned close to her. "Don't make eye contact with anyone. With luck, we'll be able to slip out without anyone else deciding to come along."

Amelia and Lord Lowenbrock met them by the garden doors. It was with disappointment that Mary released her hold on Ashford's arm and linked her arm through Amelia's. If they wanted this outing to look innocent, she and the viscount needed to appear as though their tour of the garden was going to be properly chaperoned.

A footman opened the doors, and together they escaped the gathering, Mary arm in arm with her friend while Ashford and Lowenbrock followed behind them.

Mary leaned close to Amelia. "Will anyone else be joining us?"

Amelia tilted her head in question. "I thought you and Lord Ashford wanted an opportunity to speak in private."

"We do. But it didn't occur to me that perhaps others might decide to join us."

Amelia let out a soft giggle. "Lady Herschel wanted to join us, and I might have mentioned that you have a penchant for going on long walks. I might have also laid it on a little thick, fearing that you were going to insist on leaving the grounds for a walk around the neighborhood and that, as a good host, I wouldn't be able to refuse your request."

Mary shook her head. "That was quick thinking on your part."

"You should have seen the look on her face before she pretended to hear her husband calling for her."

Mary laughed, imagining the older woman's horror at being forced to follow them. She doubted the heavyset woman had ever walked a distance farther than from a carriage to the door of whatever building she was visiting.

Amelia led them down the path to the back corner of the garden. It amazed Mary how large the garden was given the house's location. Her own sister only had a small plot of land behind her house, but her brother-in-law was only a baron. It shouldn't have surprised her that a marquess who possessed a number of estates would have a large home and private garden in the middle of London.

Her friend turned in to an alcove that Mary hadn't even seen. "This is where we'll leave you until you're ready to rejoin us. Just start back the way we've come when you're done *talking*. We'll raise the alarm if anyone has decided to follow us."

Mary held back her protest at her friend's assumptions. To do so would only make it appear that Amelia had hit on the truth.

She watched Amelia walk toward the men and murmur something to Ashford that Mary didn't catch. The viscount bowed, and their friends turned and started walking back along the path.

Ashford stepped into the small alcove, and suddenly Mary felt as though he had taken up all the air along with all the space. She'd always thought Ashford a handsome man and had noticed that his shoulders were broad, but in the small space of the garden alcove, he seemed even more imposing.

If she were with anyone other than Lord Ashford, she'd be alarmed right now.

"Congratulations, Miss Trent. You have turned one of my closest friends into one of your fiercest protectors."

"Are you referring to Lord Lowenbrock? What did he say to you?"

"Apparently he has no qualms about calling me out if I hurt you."

Mary let out a peal of laughter. "I'm sure he didn't say that. Amelia might have though. Is that what she said to you just now?"

"She was telling me that she wouldn't allow her husband to kill me because she was certain my intentions were honorable."

"I hate lying to them. Perhaps this wasn't a good idea after all."

One corner of his mouth kicked up, bringing about a corresponding jump in her heart rate. "Oh, this is definitely a bad idea."

She had to look away for a moment to gather her wits. She wouldn't allow herself to get carried away imagining things that weren't possible.

"So," he said when she didn't speak. "You asked me a question."

For a moment she wanted to take it back. Tell him that she didn't want to know. But her sister's derogatory remarks about Mary's appearance, together with Amelia's insistence that Edwina was jealous of her, had her needing to learn the truth. No matter how embarrassing she might find the answer.

She squared her shoulders and willed away her sudden desire to run from this man. But when she tried to speak, all she could manage was a quiet *yes* around her suddenly dry throat.

Ashford held his arms clasped behind his back, but something in his gaze, coupled with the privacy of their current environment, had her feeling as though he was a hair's breadth away from reaching for her.

Which was a silly thought. They were only friends.

"What do you know about kissing?"

Mary scrunched her nose, remembering the time one of the local boys at home had tried to kiss her when she was eighteen. "I know it's entirely unpleasant."

He raised a brow. "How many men have you kissed?"

Her mouth dropped open in surprise before she snapped it closed. "Just the one. And I didn't kiss him, he kissed me. The entire experience was one I didn't care to repeat."

A nerve jumped in Ashford's cheek. When he

spoke, his anger shocked her. "Did he force himself on you?"

It took her a moment to understand his meaning. Heat flooded her face. "No, of course not. He merely attempted to kiss me. It only lasted a few moments before I was able to push him away."

"Was this someone who was courting you?"

Mary lifted one shoulder in a shrug. "He was one of several men who showed interest in me. I had the misfortune of finding myself alone with him for a few minutes when I had gone out for a walk. He took the opportunity to tell me he wanted to show me the depth of his affections. Instead, I felt as though I'd been slobbered over by a very messy hound."

Ashford let out a burst of laughter.

Mary folded her arms across her chest. "It wasn't amusing."

His laughter died. "No, I imagine it wasn't. What happened with the other men?"

"They lost interest."

Ashford's brows drew together in a frown. "I find that impossible to believe."

"You've come to know me, my lord. I don't have much to recommend me. My sister said they were likely taking pity on me in the first place."

"Excuse my bluntness, but Lady Fairbanks is a lying bitch."

Mary's mouth dropped open. Then, to her horror,

she let out an indelicate snort before falling into peals of laughter.

Ashford looked at her as though she had grown two heads. "I don't think stories about your sister's cruelty toward you are amusing."

Mary swiped at her eyes as she worked to gain control of her amusement. "No, neither do I. But she would die… just die… if she knew you thought her a…" She waved a hand in his direction. "What you said."

"To be truthful, I rarely think of her at all."

"Oh, ouch! I think that would cut her even deeper."

One corner of his mouth lifted. "And what would she think if she knew the two of us were here together… for all intents and purposes, alone?"

She didn't even have to think about it. "She would hate me. Well, even more than she already does."

"Mary—"

It was the first time he'd ever called her by her Christian name, and the intimacy sent a frisson of awareness down her spine.

"Please don't concern yourself about my relationship with my sister. It was strained years ago. Likely when our parents died and she found herself needing to care for me."

"Family can be complicated, I know."

Mary's heart softened when she saw the flare of

understanding in his eyes. This man did know how she felt. "Do you wish to speak about it?"

He shook his head. "Perhaps another time. But Lowenbrock and his wife might return at any moment, and I believe there was something you wanted to know. About why your sister would tell you that your mouth is unseemly."

She nodded. "And why…" She had to clear her throat before continuing. "Why I've caught you staring at me." Her hand waved in front of her mouth.

"To begin, despite your previous experience, kissing can be quite pleasant."

"I shall have to take your word for it."

"Or I could show you. But only if you want me to."

Mary's mouth dried at the implication. Was he saying that he wanted to kiss her? And why did she not find that thought unpleasant?

"Do you trust me, Miss Trenton?"

Mary nodded without a moment's hesitation. His smile at her response felt like the highest of praise.

"To begin, one's lips are very sensitive. When one is kissed—properly and only when the lady in question desires it as much as the man—it can feel quite pleasant."

Mary sighed. Given how happy Amelia was in her marriage, she'd imagined that to be true. She also knew that kissing the man standing before her would feel very different to her last experience. But their courtship was only pretend, and he would never want to kiss her.

"Lips can also deliver a great deal of pleasure."

He extended his arm toward her. Again, without hesitation, she placed her hand in his.

He lifted her hand to his mouth, turning it so that her wrist was up. He used one gloved finger to draw down the fabric and expose her wrist. For a moment Mary forgot to breathe, only to release her breath in a loud exhale when his mouth landed softly on the skin at her wrist. The light touch of his lips against her skin, together with the warmth of his breath, sent heat coursing through her.

He straightened and gazed down at her, waiting for her reaction.

"That was quite nice." The words were a pale description of what she'd felt at the all-too-brief touch of his mouth on her skin.

His eyes seemed to bore into her. "Yes. And let me assure you, Miss Trenton, that you have a mouth made for sin."

She was beyond caring about propriety. The way he looked at her had her believing he might just grant her heart's deepest desire.

"Show me."

His gaze drifted down to her mouth before lifting again to hers. The heat reflected in his eyes made her feel as though she were the most desirable woman in all of England. Perhaps even the world.

He cleared his throat and looked away. She realized that perhaps there was a hidden meaning to her words that she didn't understand. "With a kiss, my lord. I wish to know that it can be more than what my one experience led me to believe. And unless I'm mistaken, you are the man to show me that perhaps I'm not lacking after all."

CHAPTER 14

It was impossible not to get carried away. He'd only meant to give her a light kiss, hoping it would be enough to satisfy Mary's curiosity. But when his mouth touched hers, she let out a soft sound that ignited his desire. In that moment, nothing could have stopped him from deepening the kiss.

He deserved a medal for going so slowly. When she'd caught him staring earlier, he'd been wondering what her mouth would feel like under his, and now he had the answer. He hadn't exaggerated when he told her that her mouth was made for sin. But what shocked him now was how much her lips tasted like heaven. Soft, plump, and more pliable than he had imagined.

And since he was only human, he'd imagined it quite often of late.

He swallowed her soft sound of contentment as he

brushed his mouth over hers. When he traced the seam of her lips with his tongue, she opened for him with a sigh.

He wouldn't ask who it was that had attempted to steal a kiss from her in the past. He was only grateful she'd found the entire affair distasteful enough to swear off other men. It was the height of selfishness, but no one had ever accused him of being a saint. And the way Mary returned his kiss told him she was enjoying this as much as him.

He'd planned to have just a small taste of her. Enough to satisfy the curiosity of them both. But without even realizing it, he'd drawn her into his arms. No one would describe this kiss as light or innocent.

When he started to raise his head, she made a soft sound of protest before her tongue swept into his mouth just as his had done moments before.

Just like that he was lost. Lost to desire, lost to Mary.

He pulled her closer until their bodies were flush against one another and couldn't hold back a groan. Mary wasn't a slight woman, and the way her curves pressed against him had his thoughts leaping forward to what *could* happen next.

Ruthlessly, knowing that this was neither the time nor the place to go any further, he called upon every ounce of discipline he'd developed during his years in the army and raised his head.

It took him a little longer to take a step back. They were still too close, and his hands were still cupping her face, but in that moment, he was powerless to move away.

Mary stared up at him, her breath coming in light pants and her eyes filled with wonder. If a man could grow taller from such admiration, it would have happened to him. He'd been with more women than he cared to remember, but the only person who mattered to him was Mary. He wanted to be worthy of the appreciation he saw reflected in her eyes, and he realized he might have miscalculated when starting this pretend courtship.

If he wasn't careful, he would find himself well and truly lost.

He lowered his hands, ignoring the pang of regret that slammed through him, and took another step back.

"I apologize—"

"You were correct—"

They both spoke at once and then stopped at the same time. Playing the role of gentleman that he was far from feeling, Ashford indicated that Mary should continue.

She shook her head. "I don't know why that felt so different than the last man who kissed me, but you were correct. It was… pleasant."

He felt a slight sting to his pride. "Pleasant?"

Mary's mouth firmed, and she raised one shoulder. "I suppose you have a great deal of experience in kissing."

She started to turn away, but Ashford took hold of one of her hands to keep her from hiding. "I do have some experience, yes." Her shoulders stiffened, and he couldn't let her believe that this was like all those other times. "But I can assure you that what we shared just now was no ordinary kiss."

She took a step closer, and so did he. "It wasn't?"

"No. Which is why we need to rejoin our hosts."

"Why?"

"Because, Miss Trenton, you are tempting me to distraction."

Her free hand rose to her mouth, and he wanted to groan again when he realized her lips were swollen from the kiss they'd shared. He closed his eyes, attempting to gather his scattered wits.

The sound of Amelia's laughter told him they were about to have company. He wasn't sure whether to curse Lowenbrock and his wife or thank them for the reminder that anyone could come upon them.

He released Mary's hand and offered her his arm. She took a deep breath, and he was powerless to keep his eyes from flitting to her décolletage, appreciating the way her breasts strained at the neckline of her dress. Good Lord, he needed to pull himself together.

She took his arm, and together they stepped out onto the path, just in time to see their friends come into view. No one said a word about what had just happened, and Amelia proceeded to talk about the plans Lowenbrock's sister had for improving the gardens.

He found it impossible to concentrate on her words, and he realized he had miscalculated. Was it possible that their pretend courtship was, in fact, real?

CHAPTER 15

Ashford had actually kissed her. And unlike her first and last experience kissing a man, it had been glorious.

The grin on Amelia's face when they'd joined her and Lowenbrock had her wondering if her friend knew what had happened. Could someone tell just by looking at her that her senses were now befuddled?

Amelia linked arms with her again and allowed the men to walk ahead without them. "I need to show you something."

Mary gave her head a small shake. "I'm not very good with plants."

Amelia laughed, taking her down a path that split off from the main one they'd followed to the little alcove. The alcove where Ashford had kissed her and made her want something that could never be hers. Her cheeks heated at the memory.

"John and I were surprised to find there was a gazebo in the gardens here. It's almost completely surrounded by hedges." She took hold of Mary's hand. "But you can push through here and…" She dragged Mary through a small gap in the greenery.

Once they were through the hedges, they stood before a small garden gazebo. The white structure was made of wood and wrought iron. "It's in surprisingly good shape for something long forgotten."

Mary followed her friend into the small structure. "It's very pretty."

"And there are seats along the inner railing."

Amelia seemed far too excited about the place. "Why are you showing me this?"

This time it was Amelia's turn to blush. "John and I… Well, it's very private here. We might have spent some time here since coming to London."

Mary shook her head. "Meaning what exactly?"

"It's the perfect place for a secret rendezvous. I thought I'd show it to you in case you and Lord Ashford ever find yourselves in need of a little privacy."

Mary brought her hands up to cover her face, her embarrassment acute, but she couldn't stop the barrage of images that flooded her mind. She and Ashford coming out here to be alone, and perhaps there would even be kissing.

Something had changed today. Suddenly she

found that she no longer wanted her courtship with Ashford to be pretend. But he was a man and no doubt very experienced with women. She had to remember that a kiss—even one as delightful and heated as the kiss they'd shared—would mean nothing to him.

"We should go back now," Mary said, forcing herself to meet her friend's knowing gaze.

Amelia sighed. "Of course. But I'd rather stay here and discuss what happened between you and Lord Ashford just now."

Mary wanted to confide in Amelia. If anyone could help her to understand the riot of confusion within her, it was her best friend. She'd told Ashford that she'd keep their pretend courtship a secret, but that didn't mean she had to keep everything a secret.

"He kissed me."

Amelia let out a small squeal and grasped her hands. "I told you there was something more than friendship between the two of you. Do you believe me now?"

She nodded, not wanting to damn herself with a lie. Their courtship might be pretend, but her feelings were very real.

She followed Amelia back through the garden, trying to remember the route to the gazebo. She didn't think she'd need it, but it never hurt to be prepared.

"Distract me," she said.

Amelia grinned, and Mary wanted to groan. That grin could only mean her friend was brewing up trouble.

"There's a masquerade ball next week. I need to attend… Research for my next book."

Mary's brows drew together. "Who's hosting it? I don't remember Edwina saying anything about a masked ball."

Amelia lowered her voice. "It's a public masquerade. There will be members of the demimonde there."

Mary's eyes widened. "Your husband agreed to this?"

"Of course. He didn't want to risk having me go on my own. And I want you to come with us."

Mary was intrigued. She'd heard all manner of gossip about the things that went on at such affairs. But Lowenbrock would be glued to Amelia's side. She'd have no such protection herself.

"I can ask John to invite Ashford."

And there went Mary's doubt. If Ashford was going to be there, she wanted to attend as well. There would be no need to pretend they were courting there, no one for whom they were putting on a show.

It would give her the opportunity to see how he behaved when he wasn't trying to convince his mother and sister that his interest in her was genuine. Would he still pay attention to her? Perhaps kiss her again?

Or would he use the time away from the prying eyes of the ton to dally elsewhere?

Her stomach clenched at the thought, but she had to protect her heart. Which meant she had to know Ashford's true feelings. The masquerade might be just the place to find the answers she needed.

CHAPTER 16

Mary took a deep breath as the carriage slowed to a halt outside the assembly rooms where the masquerade was being held. It was impossible to forget the image that had stared back at her in her dressing table mirror when Amelia's maid had finished dressing her. Her hair was up but the mass was very loose, the pins arranged throughout with little jewels that winked under the light. The artfully casual style gave the appearance that her hair was about to come tumbling down with the slightest shake of her head.

And her dress! It was white, but that was where the nod toward purity ended. The bodice clung to her slight curves, somehow making her bosom seem larger and in danger of falling out of her bodice. That was a look her sister had perfected, but Mary had never tried to emulate it. When she stood, the skirts fell away from the high waist in a straight line with no extra folds of fabric. Between that and the almost diaphanous material, it clung to her hips and legs as she moved.

Mary turned to Amelia, who was sitting next to her in the carriage. "I can't believe you convinced me to do this." She pinned Lowenbrock, who was sitting opposite them, with narrowed eyes. "Or that you're allowing it."

Lowenbrock shrugged. "My wife and I have an agreement. If she wants to do research for a book, she must allow me to accompany her. We both know she's going to find a way to do it with or without my permission."

"I'm sitting right here," Amelia said. But from the twinkle in her eyes, it was clear she wasn't annoyed with them. "You look beautiful, Mary. Ashford won't be able to take his eyes off you."

That made her sit up straighter. "He didn't tell me he would be here tonight."

"He has to extricate himself from a dinner his mother has arranged," Lowenbrock said. "He's not sure how long that will take."

She was torn between hope and a touch of dread and couldn't help but feel a little ridiculous in her outfit. The circlet of flowers Amelia had woven into her hair just before they'd left the house, telling her that tonight she would be Venus, the goddess of love, made her feel like a little girl playing dress-up.

Amelia and her husband were dressed as Cupid and Psyche.

Lowenbrock helped them both down from the carriage, and together they made their way into the large building. It was already midnight, and from the music and raucous sound of voices wafting outside, the masquerade was well underway.

Lowenbrock had agreed to accompany his wife and her friend to the public ball that everyone knew would be frequented by members of the demimonde, but he'd already warned Amelia that they wouldn't be staying until dawn, when the masquerade would draw to a close. He'd agreed to two hours only, after which he was whisking them away to safety.

They stood on the edge of the ballroom, taking in the masked figures that crowded the room. Mary couldn't help but note the double standard that seemed to exist. Amelia was dressed in a similar fashion to her, but Lowenbrock looked much like he always did at each of their evening entertainments. She'd thought he was being stubborn and refusing to wear a costume. But it was clear that many of the men present wore their normal evening attire, added a domino or full face mask, and declared themselves dressed for the masquerade. The fairer sex, on the other hand, all wore the flimsiest of gowns, which clung to their bodies.

As she took in the beautiful women that surrounded them, some with slits in their dresses cut indecently high, she couldn't help but hope Ashford wouldn't make an appearance. What had seemed like an ordinary event on the surface took on darker undertones as she caught sight of women and men tucked away into small alcoves that were situated around the perimeter of the large ballroom.

Amelia was trying to take in everything at once, her eyes wide as she looked around the room. Mary was surprised her friend hadn't already taken out the notebook Mary knew she was carrying in her reticule and started scribbling down notes on the scandalous scenes that played out before them.

Lowenbrock's posture was tense, but he kept an arm firmly around his wife, allowing Mary to take his other arm. That he was with two women wouldn't raise eyebrows here, not when Mary had seen two men escorting a young woman to one of the alcoves.

Mary's eyes skittered away from that scene when they began pressing their mouths to the woman's exposed skin, their hands roaming over her body, without even closing the curtain that hung to one side!

She turned her gaze toward the middle of the room, hoping there would be less shocking events taking place there. And, of course, caught sight of Ashford on the far side of the room. Her mind blanked when she realized he was striding in their direction.

In a panic, she released the marquess's arm and took a step back, thinking only that she needed to get out of that room. Amelia's arm on her elbow brought her to a halt.

"Where do you think you're going? Do you want one of these other men to grab you and take you away? Because that could very well happen if you leave us."

"Ashford is here, and he's headed this way. How did I ever allow you to talk me into this?" She lowered her voice so she wouldn't be overheard. "I feel as though I'm not wearing any clothes."

Amelia's eyes danced with merriment behind her white mask. "I hate to tell you this, but I don't think the sight of a female body is going to be a shock to Ashford's sensibilities."

Mary didn't like the images that sprang to mind at her friend's statement. She knew Ashford was worldly and imagined that he'd experienced far more than she could imagine. But just thinking about him in the arms of another woman, especially after the kiss they'd shared, made her heart ache. She didn't want to examine why that would be the case since the man wasn't hers. He could be with any woman he wanted.

"Ladies. My lord."

Mary's eyes closed for a second before she braced herself and turned around. Ashford's eyes were on hers and… Yes, there it was. He swept his gaze over her body. But instead of feeling as though she were going to die of embarrassment, a different sort of heat began to work its way through her. Especially when he met her gaze again and she saw the heat of awareness reflected there.

CHAPTER 17

Tension fell away from him, and for the first time since his mother had arrived in town, Ashford felt as though he could finally take a full breath. If he ran into anyone he knew here tonight, they wouldn't say a word. There would be no gossip, no staring, no speculation about his courtship of Miss Trenton. The unwritten rule of the night was that no one shared what they saw or heard.

Of course, Lowenbrock's wife would be breaking that rule if she wrote about this—or a similar masquerade—in an upcoming book. But she wouldn't be sharing names, and that was all anyone cared about.

The assembly rooms were already crowded, and the press of bodies would only get worse as the night progressed. There hadn't been any question that he would move heaven and earth to be here. He wouldn't miss the chance to see Mary without the eyes of the ton on them. One week had passed since he'd kissed her, and with any luck, he'd be able to do so again tonight.

He prowled around the outskirts of the room, scanning those assembled. When he couldn't find Mary, he kept his gaze on the main doors to the ballroom. He spotted the tall, fair-haired Lowenbrock and the two women he escorted as soon as they stepped into the room. Satisfaction surged when his gaze locked on Mary's, and he started toward them. The red mask she wore over the upper part of her face did little to disguise her identity.

He quickened his pace when it looked as though she wanted to flee.

"Ladies. My lord," he said when he reached the group.

Lowenbrock and his wife greeted him, and he waited for Mary to turn and do the same. When she did, a shock of awareness went through him.

Of their own volition, his eyes swept over her form, taking in the dress that did nothing to hide her curves. He battled the urge to rip off his coat and cover her form so others wouldn't see her this way. When he was able to force his gaze up again, her cheeks were tinged with red. He was behaving like a brute, but it was impossible to keep hedonistic images from flooding his mind, thoughts of taking Mary into one of the many shadowy hideaways that were designed for the sole purpose of giving people the privacy they needed to give in to their baser natures.

The sound of Lowenbrock clearing his throat brought him to his senses.

"My lady," Ashford said, preserving her anonymity amongst those pressing closely. "Would you do me the honor of dancing with me?"

A smile broke over her face, and she placed her hand in his. Without a word to Lowenbrock, he tucked her hand into his arm and led her to the center of the ballroom floor.

Tonight no one would gossip if they danced more than twice together, which was a good thing because he wasn't letting this woman out of his arms.

After two lively quadrilles, he escorted her to a refreshment table for a drink. He ignored the overtures from other women, the way several of them reached out to run a hand over his arms, his back… anywhere they could reach. It was much harder to ignore the way other men looked at Mary. He tucked her close to his side and snarled at one man who'd raised a hand to touch her hair.

Her eyes widened in surprise. "Did you just… growl?"

He could only shake his head, wondering how she hadn't noticed the way men were leering at her. He'd do much worse than growl if they came any closer.

About ten minutes later, his patience was finally

rewarded when he heard the opening strains of a waltz.

Her eyes lit. "Do we dare dance together again?"

"Just try to stop me."

She laughed, and soon she was in his arms. He pulled her close, much closer than he would have been able to anywhere else. When she smiled up at him in response and pressed her body fully against him, he completely forgot about anyone else there.

He didn't care who saw him sweeping his hand down her back before finally resting it just above her backside.

"You are very wicked, my lord."

Good heavens, was this woman trying to undo the last of his self-control?

He ignored the hissed exclamation that came from behind him, assuming it was meant for someone else, until a hand on his arm attempted to pull him away from her. He tensed and turned, moving her behind him at the same time. He would battle anyone foolish enough to try to take her away from him.

The man was shorter than him, fair-haired and stocky. Ashford had never seen him before, but the man's cheeks were bright red with anger. Then, in the next second, the color drained from his face. It would have been comical if every muscle in Ashford's body wasn't tensed in preparation for a physical battle.

"You're not Henry." The man shook his head.

"You're his brother, I presume. The new Viscount Ashford. I apologize for my rudeness."

The man turned to leave, and it took Ashford's befuddled senses a moment to realize what was happening. "Wait. Please don't go." He turned to Mary. "I need to speak to him."

"Of course," she said, her eyes soft with concern. Damn, did she know about his estrangement with his brother?

He took her to Lowenbrock and Amelia, feeling a twinge of guilt at interrupting their waltz. "You need to look after Miss Trenton for me. I'll be back shortly."

His friend nodded. "Nothing will happen to her."

He hated to leave her, but at least she would be in good hands. He made his way back to the stranger. Thankfully the man hadn't fled.

"If you think to separate us, you're wasting your time." His voice was strong, confident, but there was something in the slope of the man's shoulders that gave him an air of wary resignation.

Everything clicked into place then. Why his brother hadn't moved into his town house and gone along with their father's plans to position Henry as the next viscount as he waited for his oldest son to die in battle. Why his mother and sister insisted Henry had never wanted to usurp Ashford's place. Why his mother had insisted his younger brother wouldn't be fathering the next heir. And most importantly, why she'd told him the future of the title depended solely on Ashford marrying.

"You are…"

"His lover, yes." The man let out a resigned sigh. "We can leave for France by the end of the week. If you would turn a blind eye until then, we'd be forever in your debt."

Ashford shook his head. "I'm not going to send you away."

The man blanched. "So you plan to turn us in."

"I was in the army. When you have that many men quartered together, you see all manner of things. So no, I will not be turning you in."

The man nodded. "I'll leave you to your entertainments then. I apologize for disturbing you."

Panic took hold when this stranger—his last tie to his brother—began to turn away. He couldn't help but fear that if this man left now, he and his brother could very well flee to France, fearing for their safety.

"Tell me where Henry is. I need to see him. To make things right between us."

The man shook his head.

"Please. I give you my word that no harm will come to either of you."

He waited, watching the silent battle that played out on the other man's face. Finally the man reached into an inner coat pocket and pulled out a calling card. His jaw was tight as a handed it to Ashford. "If you hurt him, you'll have to answer to me."

Ashford nodded. "Understood."

He stood there for several moments, watching as the man turned and then melted into the crowd. He hadn't even thought to ask him his name. He'd have to remedy that when he saw his brother tomorrow. This man had been there for Henry when his own family hadn't been, and for that Ashford owed him.

He made his way back to Mary, frowning when he saw that no less than three men were now hovering around her. They were speaking to Lowenbrock, but their attention was divided between Mary and Lowenbrock's wife.

As though sensing his gaze, Mary looked his way. With a word to the small group, she excused herself and came to him. Three sets of eyes followed the sway of her hips.

She placed a hand on his arm when she reached his side. "How are you? Is everything all right?"

He wanted to draw her into a hug. Instead, he placed a hand over hers. "Not yet, but it will be soon."

Her brows drew together. "Do you wish to speak about it? Amelia told me that you and your brother are estranged."

He smiled down at her, touched by her concern. "I'd rather talk about you and me. I hate that we missed the rest of the waltz." And just when it was beginning to get interesting. He didn't say the words aloud, but it was clear she was thinking the same thing.

She glanced to the left. “There’s an alcove just over there that appears to be empty.”

He took her arm in his and led her in that direction. Restraint be damned. It had been a long week since he’d last kissed this woman, and he didn’t want to wait another moment. He drew her into the small, dimly lit space, and pulled the curtain closed behind them. A candle on a high shelf provided just enough illumination to keep the alcove from falling into darkness.

No words were needed. They moved into one another’s arms as though they’d done this a hundred times before. She rose onto her toes and he leaned down, and then he was kissing her.

Before he could get carried away, he pulled back and drew her into a hug. He needed this. He needed *her*, but he was not going to take her innocence at a public masquerade.

They stood like that, leaning against one another for comfort, for at least a full minute before Mary’s voice broke into the silence.

“Amelia and Lord Lowenbrock have a gazebo in their back garden…”

CHAPTER 18

No power on earth could have kept him away. He didn't know what love was, but he knew about compatibility. Mary Trenton was level-headed, and her background made her suitable for any member of the ton. Her sharp wit and keen observations amused him. Beyond that, he liked and respected her a great deal.

And there was no denying her beauty. His feelings for her had quickly grown from mere friendship—how could they not? He'd seen the way other men looked at her. After he'd made his own interest in her known, they'd started sniffing around her for themselves. The thought that one of those men might win her heart had his stomach clenching in knots.

He lusted after her. He hadn't expected to, but the all-too-brief kisses they'd shared had awoken an ache within him that had grown each day.

He couldn't imagine wanting to make another woman his viscountess.

If he were a better man, he'd play the part of the honorable gentleman he was supposed to be. But Mary's invitation had chased away any vague notions he might have had about behaving honorably. No, if Mary Trenton wanted to know what it would be like to be intimate with a man, he'd show her. And then he would do everything possible to secure her hand.

He slipped around the side of the house, hoping no one would mistake him for a thief, and headed toward the back of the garden. They hadn't made it this far during their quick tour the other day, but it wasn't hard to find. The very top of the gazebo's roof peeked out over a row of tall hedges. He had no idea what kind they were, but they would provide a measure of privacy. Just enough for him to show Mary that he could take her to heights of pleasure using just his hands and mouth.

He made his way down the row of hedges, a slight frown creasing his brow. Had he gone the wrong way? But then he saw the barely visible gap between the dense shrubs.

He froze when he caught sight of her. She was sitting on one of the stone benches that seemed to line the interior of the gazebo. She sat facing his direction, but her eyes were closed. He took in the sight of her white nightdress. Her unbound hair, which appeared darker under the illumination of the moon, fell around her shoulders almost to her waist. His hands clenched with the need to bury his fingers in that mass.

She opened her eyes then and their gazes met.

Silence stretched between them for several long seconds before he stepped into the gazebo and crossed the small distance between them.

Mary rose to her feet, her hands clasped together at her waist. She looked up at him and shook her head. "I didn't think you'd come."

Disappointment crashed through him at the cool note in her voice, but he would never force himself on her. He took hold of one of her hands, delighting in the way her smaller, bare fingers felt in his. "How could I resist such an invitation? But if you've changed your mind…"

Her head tilted to one side as her eyes searched his. She took a deep breath, and he had to force himself not to look down at her chest. The bodice of her nightdress was more modest than the gown she'd worn earlier that night, but the knowledge that she was clad simply in her sleep clothes had his senses on high alert.

"I haven't changed my mind."

He let out the breath he'd been holding. Pulling her closer, he stared down at her, searching for any hint of hesitation on her part. When she bit down on her lower lip, he wanted to groan. Instead, he cupped her chin in one hand and drew his thumb along the soft plumpness of her lips.

She closed her eyes and nuzzled into his touch. Sending up a silent thank-you to the heavens above, he lowered his mouth to hers.

He wanted to go slowly, had planned to, but all caution fled when she pressed herself against him. The feel of her soft breasts against his chest, bare of any restraining corset, had him wanting to take everything she would give him.

She opened her mouth in invitation, and he delved in. Their tongues battled, soft sounds of contentment coming from the back of Mary's throat and echoing against his own groan of relief.

He wrenched his mouth away and stared down at her for several long seconds. When her heavy-lidded gaze met his, he lifted her into his arms.

She let out a soft gasp and twined her hands around his neck. "I'm too heavy—"

"Nonsense," he said, turning them so he could lower himself onto the bench where Mary had waited for him minutes before. He settled her across his lap. Much as he wanted her to straddle him, he wouldn't rush this.

Her face was buried against his shoulder. "I can't believe we're doing this."

He forced himself to say, "I will stop at any point if you change your mind."

By way of reply, she swept her tongue along the

edge of his cravat before reaching out to tug at the knot. It came undone with only a few deft movements of her clever fingers.

"I've always wondered what a man's whiskers felt like." She brushed her face alongside his. "I think I like it."

Images of brushing those same whiskers along her breasts and the skin of her thighs flooded his mind. Restraint was going to be harder than he'd imagined. "You make it almost impossible to behave like a gentleman."

She pulled back and gazed up at him, a slight frown appearing between her brows. "I thought the idea was for you *not* to be a gentleman."

He closed his eyes, trying to ignore the invitation in her words. His tenuous grasp on restraint was quickly fraying.

"Of course, if you think I should ask someone else…"

And just like that it snapped.

CHAPTER 19

Her hollow threat had worked. She had no intention of approaching another man and asking him to make love to her. She could scarce believe she was even asking Ashford. No other man had ever stirred such feelings in her. Desire, admiration… and trust. She trusted him.

Ashford lifted her, and for a moment she thought he was going to set her on her feet. Her disappointment vanished, however, when he brought her down over his lap again, but this time her legs were draped on each side of his.

Her nightdress rose, exposing her lower legs to the cool night air. She should be shocked, but instead a thrill of anticipation filled her.

"You have no idea what you're asking for."

"I think I do, my lord. Amelia has… shared a few things with me."

He closed his eyes again, which meant he was trying to gain a measure of control. She couldn't have that. She wanted this man out of control.

His hands on her hips kept her perched over his knees. With a deep breath, she inched closer to him. His eyes sprang open, and the heat reflected within them gave her the confidence she needed to continue.

He helped her, one strong hand on her back, the other still clutching her hip, as he brought her body fully against him.

The shock of sensation was like nothing she'd ever felt before. If she thought the way her breasts felt when she was pressed against his firm chest was shocking, it was nothing compared to the way his hard length felt between her legs, where no one had ever touched her.

He was hard for her, a sign that her friend had assured her meant he very much wanted to make love to her.

She rubbed herself against him, enjoying the way he growled almost as much as she enjoyed the shock of sensation that went through her.

"This is your last chance to change your mind." His voice was rough, his jaw clenched, telling her how much he, too, wanted to continue.

In reply, she brought her mouth to his.

Thankfully, Ashford took charge then. She cried out in protest when he ended the kiss before she was ready, but instead of pushing her away as she'd feared he was about to do, he brought his mouth to the side of her throat.

Delicious shivers flowed through her as he continued a heated path to the neckline of her nightdress. With a quick movement, he dragged the fabric down over her shoulders and exposed her breasts to the night air.

If she'd had any reservations before he arrived, they were well and truly gone now. The fact that they could be discovered only added to her excitement. She didn't want to think about what that said about her.

His mouth covered one nipple, pulling on it, while he weighed the other breast with a hand. And through it all, his other hand kept her pressed tightly to his rigid length. The tumult of sensation was almost too much.

And then he started moving. Or, more accurately, he started rocking her along his length. When she realized what he wanted, she began to rise up and down as best she could, her feet just reaching the ground as she perched on his lap. She dropped her face into the crook of his neck, her breath coming in harsh pants, echoing with his own.

She didn't know what happened, but she went from enjoying the feelings he was wringing from her body to being desperate for more. If he stopped now, she didn't think she'd recover.

And then something wonderful happened. A wave

of pleasure streaked through her body, almost too much to bear. She started to cry out, but he captured her mouth with his, swallowing the sound.

They stilled, his hard length still pressed against her. And then he pushed her back until she was perched on his knees. She felt the loss of his body against hers keenly.

His breath was still harsh, whereas hers was starting to calm, and she realized that whatever pleasure he'd just given her, he'd denied himself the same.

She examined him. His eyes were closed, his jaw clenched, confirming her suspicion.

Amelia had told her there were things a man and a woman could do outside the marriage bed to bring pleasure to one another, but she hadn't given Mary any details. Well, she'd now experienced one of those things, and she wanted to give Ashford his own release.

Clinging only to the fact that he had pushed her away from him, she surmised that the feel of her body against his had brought him to the brink of losing control. His hands pressed firmly on her hips, preventing her from sliding close to him again. So instead, she reached down, hoping that he would enjoy her touch on his member. Perhaps it would help him find his own satisfaction.

His hand wrapped around her wrist and his eyes fixed on hers for what seemed like an eternity. Finally he swore and lifted her from his lap. She found herself sitting on the bench, watching in stunned silence while he stood and turned away from her.

What should she do?

She raised a hand to reach out to him again and hesitated. Which was silly, really, given what had just happened between them.

If she leaned forward, she'd be able to touch his backside, which was covered by his black tailcoat. She almost diverted her hand to his waist, but her hesitation was absurd since he'd kissed her breasts. Her naked breasts.

Heat colored her cheeks while she brought the fabric of her nightdress back over her shoulders to cover herself again. Then, with a confidence she was far from feeling, she placed her hand on his backside.

His reaction was instant. He stiffened before turning to face her again, making sure to step back far enough so she couldn't touch him. But she could clearly see that he was still hard, which meant he didn't want to stop.

She took a deep breath, noticing the way his eyes traveled down to her now-covered breasts, and stood. His eyes, when they met hers again, were filled with heat.

She licked her lips, and he actually groaned. "We don't need to stop—"

"I will not take your innocence in a garden."

"But—"

"We were fortunate no one came upon us."

"Amelia assured me it would be safe. She and her husband have…" She couldn't actually say it. It was bad enough she knew what her friend and her husband had done out here. And now she'd told Ashford.

He closed his eyes and took a deep breath. "I'll pretend I don't know that."

"What we've done tonight… I know there's more. I want to share that with you. Now more than ever."

His stare bored into her and she met it, refusing to look away. She wouldn't be embarrassed. What had happened between them was more special than she could have imagined. When this season was over, she was going to retire to the country. She wouldn't apologize for wanting a taste of the pleasure that could be found between a man and a woman. Because one thing was now abundantly clear to her. She could never share such intimacies with another man.

He reached for her hand, taking it between his. There was something in his gaze that had her heart soaring.

"I've been thinking that perhaps it is time to end our pretense."

And just like that, her foolish hopes came crashing back to earth. He didn't want her in that way. She'd been a disappointment to him.

She tugged her hand from his grasp and took a step back. Ashford waited patiently for her response.

"I understand, and I apologize for imposing on you in this manner."

His brows drew together. "What do you mean?"

She waved a hand toward the bench where he had shown her a glimpse of the pleasure that would never again be hers.

"I apologize for being selfish. I will let Amelia know that our courtship is over. I'll also tell your sister that the decision was mine the next time we meet. That I changed my mind. It is, after all, a woman's prerogative."

She started to turn away, hoping to flee back to the house before tears of hurt and humiliation could fall. His hand on her arm halted her progress.

He turned her to face him, his eyes roaming over her face. "I have made a mess of this. I wasn't saying that we should end our courtship. Just the pretense."

It took several seconds for the meaning of his words to sink in. His expression was so serious that she thought she might have heard him wrong.

"I don't understand. You're saying…"

One corner of his mouth lifted, and with that a portion of her heart began to lighten. "That what is happening between us is more than just pretend."

She shook her head, unable to believe she'd heard him correctly. "I think I might be dreaming. I am in bed right now, imagining that I came down to the garden to meet you."

He chuckled. "Oh, you definitely came down to

meet me, and you tempted me beyond words. So much so that you've convinced me the only person I was fooling with this pretend courtship was myself."

This wasn't actually happening. Ashford wanted to court her? Did he have feelings for her? Did she have feelings for him? Was her earlier disappointment due to more than just embarrassment?

"You mean to say…" She wouldn't act the coward now, but she had to take a deep breath before continuing. "You want to court me in earnest?"

"Would that be so hard to believe?"

"Frankly, yes. There are far more suitable women than me."

"You forget that I've seen what the ton has to offer. Yet I chose to court you."

She shook her head, unable to believe she wasn't dreaming. "You chose to pretend to court me. There is a vast difference between courting a woman you are interested in marrying and asking one to help you remain unattached."

His eyes held a hint of regret. "I never meant to insult you."

She shook her head. "You didn't insult me, my lord. I was never under any illusion that someone like you would want to marry someone like me."

His eyes narrowed. "Someone like you?"

"Someone far too old and only passably attractive."

She let out a soft cry of surprise when he clasped her by the upper arms and pulled her against him.

"Stop being so hard on yourself. Those are your sister's words. I can assure you that you are more than passably attractive."

Her mouth twisted at the tepid compliment. "Oh yes, my too-wide mouth makes you think about kissing me."

"Your mouth, my dear, has men thinking about having you drag it all over their bodies." He must have seen her confusion because he took hold of one of her hands and brought it to his hardness. "Most especially here."

Her mind blanked at the image his words conjured. Then, almost of their own volition, her fingers curled around his length. Is that what men wanted from a woman? She remembered how good it had felt to have his mouth on her breast, pulling the tip into its warmth. Would he enjoy it if she took his hard length into her mouth? She should be slapping him right now, but instead she found herself wanting to do what she had just imagined.

He placed his hand over hers and lifted it to his mouth, dropping a kiss into her palm. "You would test the patience of a saint. And I am no saint."

The promise in his words had heat beginning to unfurl within her again. "So…"

"So I need to take my leave now before this goes any further tonight."

His words disappointed her, but at least he wasn't saying this would be the end of their time together.

She raised one brow and leaned closer into him, enjoying the way her overly sensitive breasts felt pressed against his muscular chest. "Tomorrow?"

He let out a short bark of laughter before capturing her mouth in a heated kiss. All too soon it was over and he pushed her away.

She frowned in disappointment.

"Tomorrow I will begin to show you that I meant what I said. I wish to court you in earnest, Mary Trenton."

And with that he strode away from the gazebo and passed through the break in the hedge that hid the little structure.

Mary clasped her upper arms and let out a soft sigh, allowing herself to give in to the thread of hope beginning to grow within her.

CHAPTER 20

After returning home, Ashford's frustration at leaving Mary before he'd found his own release had him taking himself in hand to ease the ache. It wasn't the same as being with her, but it helped to give him clarity.

He'd meant it when he told her he wanted to court her in earnest. But before he could move on with his future, he needed to set aside past hurts. He needed to see his brother.

He sent a note to Henry at first light and then waited, pacing in his room. His mother would assume he was still asleep after being out for most of the night and so wouldn't expect him to come down for breakfast, which suited him just fine. He couldn't help but wonder how much his mother knew about Henry's life. She must have at least suspected the reason he'd disappeared given her veiled comments about how her younger son wouldn't be producing the next heir. Which left the question about why she hadn't told him. Ashford could only hope it wasn't because she thought he might do something to hurt his brother.

But hadn't he done just that when he'd allowed their father to drive a wedge between them? Shame filled him that he'd waited so long to seek Henry out. That feeling only grew when a message from his brother arrived, saying he would expect him later that morning.

It was still early, but he couldn't go back to sleep. Which meant he had nothing to do but pace and wait.

After an interminable few hours, he finally set out for his brother's house. He didn't know London well enough to recognize the address, and he feared that his brother was living in an unsafe part of town. That fear was put to rest when the carriage slowed in front of a modest house in a genteel neighborhood.

He lifted the knocker, and the door was opened moments later by the man he'd met the previous evening. The man wore house livery, which told him he was either Henry's butler or he had taken on that role to keep the neighbors from suspecting the truth about their relationship. It wouldn't be safe for either man if rumors spread that they were lovers, and they would face the very real threat of being jailed.

Ashford extended a hand, opting for a casual introduction. "I think we started out on the wrong foot yesterday. I am Anthony Ashford."

"William Benson," the man said, but instead of taking Ashford's hand, he folded his arms across his chest. A vee formed between his brows, the corners of his mouth turning down. "I'll be watching you."

Ashford nodded and dropped his hand.

"Are you playing nice, William?"

Benson's jaw clenched as the voice came from the back of the house. He stepped aside to allow him to pass. But before Ashford did, he put an arm on Benson's shoulder. "Thank you for watching out for my brother. I am here to mend fences, not cause him any more pain."

Benson nodded, his body relaxing slightly.

Ashford started down the hall, but before he'd made it more than a few steps, his brother stepped out from the shadows.

It had been well over a decade since he'd last seen Henry, and it was a shock to see he was now a grown man. His fair hair had darkened in that time and was now a light brown color, only slightly lighter than Ashford's. Father would have been annoyed. He'd always liked that Henry had inherited his blond hair.

Henry had broadened as well, though not as much as Ashford, which was only to be expected since he hadn't spent the past decade exerting himself physically. But aside from that, it was as though Ashford were looking into a mirror. It was no wonder Benson had mistaken him for his brother.

Henry spoke first. "I think this meeting requires a drink."

It was just before noon, but Ashford heartily concurred.

He followed his brother to a room at the back of the house, which turned out to be both a library and a music room. Henry had always enjoyed playing the pianoforte, and Ashford wasn't surprised to see that instrument standing proudly in the center of the room.

He waited as Henry poured two small measures of brandy and handed him a glass. His brother eyed him with caution as he said, "To what should we drink?"

Ashford raised his glass. "To reconciliations."

Henry nodded and tossed back his drink.

He raised a brow before doing the same. His brother dropped into a chair and he took the one opposite. "You look well."

"As do you," Henry said.

One corner of his mouth lifted. "Father wouldn't have been pleased."

Henry shook his head. "I never understood why he drove you away. If I did or said anything that caused him to favor me..." He shook his head. "I hated the way he divided us. I only ever looked up to you."

Ashford leaned forward. "I am here to apologize. Looking back, I can see now that you never showed any sign of wanting to take my place as heir. Yet I allowed him to twist everything. To make me believe it would be better for everyone if you were viscount."

"He hated that you looked so much like our mother. Whereas I..." He waved a hand at his hair. "Well, I was fair and to him that meant I was clearly his son."

Ashford shook his head. "I never realized just how much we looked alike."

Henry was silent for a long moment. "There is something more."

The expression on his brother's face had Ashford's senses on high alert. "Do I want to know this?"

Henry's smile held more than a hint of sadness. "Well, you already know about my lifestyle."

"That you prefer to be with men. That became obvious to me when Benson approached me last night at the masquerade."

His brother's gaze was intent. "And that doesn't anger you?"

Ashford shrugged. "I was in the army, Henry. It was impossible for men to hide such things for long."

Henry's jaw clenched. "I would have thought men such as I would have been shot rather than be allowed to pollute His Majesty's armies."

"Not on my watch. One of the best men I've ever known gave his life to save mine. Who he chose to spend his personal time with had no bearing whatsoever on his merit."

"Father was beyond angry when he found out."

Henry's words had him reeling back. "He knew?"

"It was a few years after you enlisted. William was a footman at the estate. Father found us together."

Ashford closed his eyes, the scene vivid in his mind. Their father was not a tolerant man.

"I'm sorry you had to go through that alone. What did he do?"

Henry shrugged. "He kicked me out of the house after he had me promise not to tell Mother or our sisters. But he did arrange for a small allowance so I wasn't reduced to begging in the streets."

Ashford could only shake his head, unsure he'd heard his brother correctly. "That doesn't sound at all like our father."

"Yes, well, it turns out that Father had that same… fondness for men. And he feared you might as well, which is why he never liked the idea of your becoming the next viscount."

His whole world turned upside down with that revelation. In a way it made sense. He'd seen men overcompensate to hide their natures. And if Father… Well, that would explain why he was so strict. Why he hated the idea of Ashford inheriting.

"He told me once he hated the fact that, as heir, I was expected to go away to Eton."

"Yes, which was probably why he had me tutored

at home. I imagine he hoped that if he kept me away from other boys and young men, I wouldn't develop what he called his curse."

Ashford leaned forward and placed a hand on his brother's knee. "It's a hard life, but from the look of things, you've found a good man."

Henry placed his hand over his brother's and squeezed. "Yes. William was beside himself last night, worried his rash actions might have led to you shunning me. He knew that I'd always hoped we would one day reconcile."

"Never again, brother. Now call in Benson. I'd like to get to know the man who was there for you when I... when the entire family wasn't."

Henry's grin lit up the room. They both stood and embraced. Ashford couldn't remember the last time, if ever, he had felt this close to his brother.

"Come into the back garden. William is probably murdering the rosebushes in an attempt to distract himself while we talk. I made him promise not to hover outside the door."

Ashford laughed as he followed his brother into the small garden.

CHAPTER 21

One week had passed since Ashford's world changed. One week ago, he'd reconciled with his brother and begun the process of bringing him back into the familial fold.

It had also been seven long days and nights since he'd told Mary that he planned to court her in earnest. After the intimate activities they'd shared in the gazebo, he couldn't trust himself to be alone with her. He was trying to court her properly, but he suspected he was making a hash of things. Because with every passing day, he could feel Mary pulling away from him.

He missed her. Seeing her for a few hours each evening wasn't enough. He'd intended to wait until the end of the season before asking for her hand, but his patience was already fraying at the edges. There had been two balls, one rout, and one night at the theater. The other evenings he'd gone to Lowenbrock's house for dinner and a quiet evening. But during those three evenings, he'd wanted nothing more than to take Mary to that private gazebo again and finish what they'd started. His self-control was almost nonexistent at this point.

Before he asked for Mary's hand, he wanted to speak to Lowenbrock. Mary was of age, so he didn't need her family's permission to propose, but she was under the marquess's protection. They might be friends, but he knew Lowenbrock was very protective of the women in his life. He'd earned the nickname of Sir Galahad during the years they'd served together because he'd always been the first man to come to a woman's rescue. That propensity toward overprotectiveness now extended to Mary.

His decision made, he drove his phaeton to White's that afternoon. In the morning room, he found Cranston and Lowenbrock were already there. He crossed the room to the fireplace on the far wall, greeting others along the way, before dropping into one of the seats next to his friends.

Cranston waved to one of the footmen and asked him to bring another cup of coffee for Ashford.

"I'm glad the two of you are already here," Ashford said.

Cranston raised a brow. "I'm sure John will be rushing home to his new wife soon."

"Amelia is busy today," Lowenbrock said with a shrug. "She told me not to hurry home."

The footman brought him a cup of the strong coffee Ashford had developed a taste for while serving on the continent.

"So tell us about Miss Trenton," Cranston said.

It was a miracle the man hadn't teased him about Mary before now. Had he sensed that Ashford's feelings for her had changed? For a man who was determined never to trust a woman with his heart, he was adept at detecting the softening emotions of others.

"What's there to tell? You already know I'm courting her, and I was under the impression that you liked her."

"She's attractive, yes, and not given to frivolities. But shackling yourself to one woman?" He shuddered. "I thought you had better sense than that."

Lowenbrock let out a snort. "Don't you get tired of flitting around from woman to woman?"

Cranston's shrugged. "There's nothing wrong with having a little fun."

"I'm having a great deal of fun with my wife."

Lowenbrock's grin caused a slight tinge of jealousy to go through Ashford. That was a first. He'd never envied his friend's happy marriage, but now, with Mary, he very much wanted that for himself.

"Yes, well, not all of us are ready to settle down." Cranston turned to him again. "Which brings me back to my question. What are your intentions toward Miss Trenton? Are you actually going to marry her?"

It was time to come clean with his friends. Tell them everything and hope they wouldn't judge him too harshly. Well, Cranston wouldn't, but Lowenbrock might, especially if he thought Ashford was toying with Mary's emotions.

It occurred to him then that the man might already know. Mary might have confided in Lady Lowenbrock about their pretend courtship.

"Mary and I came to an agreement at the beginning of the season."

Lowenbrock's jaw tightened, telling Ashford that his assumption had been correct. He knew. Furthermore, his friend didn't approve.

Cranston let out a low whistle. "So you're serious. Lady Fairbanks is going to be most displeased."

The statement caught Ashford off guard. He hadn't spoken about Mary's sister to anyone. "What do you mean?"

Cranston shrugged. "She's been telling everyone that you're a blackguard and have been trifling with her sister."

A haze of anger swept over him.

Lowenbrock let out a huff of annoyance. "It's all pretend. Ashford and Miss Trenton are pretending to be courting to keep his mother from forcing him into an unwanted match." He turned to meet Ashford's frown. "Don't glare at me like that. You should have known Miss Trenton wouldn't be able to keep it a secret from her closest friend forever. She only confided in Amelia recently."

The expression on Cranston's face was almost comical. Then he slapped his knee and let out a relieved laugh. "Well, thank heavens for that."

Ashford had never wanted to punch his friend before.

Lowenbrock settled back in his chair, arms across his chest. "When the season ends with no betrothal, Lady Fairbanks will have won."

Cranston smirked. "I must say your plan was brilliant. And the rumors that woman is spreading will save you from having to enter into a similar ruse next year. No one will want their daughters to suffer a similar fate of being led astray all season."

It was clear from the tic in Lowenbrock's jaw that Ashford wasn't the only one who wanted to hit Cranston.

Cranston scowled at Lowenbrock. "Not everyone is meant for fairy-tale endings."

Ashford thought he detected a hint of bitterness in the man's words, but Cranston's expression betrayed nothing. For the first time, Ashford found himself wondering if his friend's cavalier attitude toward the fairer sex had its roots in a past heartbreak.

He detected movement out of the corner of his eye and turned to see the Marquess of Overlea stopping next to them along with his good friend the Earl of

Kerrick. It never ceased to amaze him that Lowenbrock was linked by marriage to two of the most respected members of the ton. When they'd been in the army together, John had never let on that his sister was married to a marquess. He'd simply told them his family was impoverished to the point that his commission had been purchased by a family friend. Ashford had known the man several years before he learned both his sisters were married, one to a marquess and one to an earl.

And then the letter had arrived to tell him he'd inherited the title of Marquess of Lowenbrock. John had been convinced it wasn't real, actually going so far as to say that his eldest sister had likely invented the fiction to entice him to return to England.

But it became clear it was no joke when all the other officers began to treat John differently.

Overlea clapped Lowenbrock on the shoulder and dipped his head in greeting to him and Cranston before he and Kerrick moved past them to take a seat by the bow window that overlooked Saint James Street.

Lowenbrock rose from his seat. "I need to speak to them. I'll be right back."

Ashford and Cranston watched their friend join his brothers-in-law.

Cranston shook his head. "I still can't believe the ne'er-do-well is so well connected."

"Or that he now outranks us."

Cranston let out a snort and drained the rest of his coffee.

The conversation quieted, and the whole room seemed to still. They turned to see the Earl of Brantford and the Duke of Clarington had entered the room. The duke went to join his good friends by the window, ruffling John's hair before settling into a chair. John scowled at the man but greeted him warmly.

Ashford turned back to Cranston, about to say something about how their positions in society were firmly cemented thanks to their friendship with the new Marquess of Lowenbrock. His flippant remark died when he saw that the Earl of Brantford had joined them.

One look from the earl was all it took for Cranston to rise to his feet. With a nod, he turned and made his way to the group by the bow window.

Brantford took the seat Cranston had vacated.

Ashford knew the man only by reputation. Lowenbrock had said something about how Kerrick knew him and that he'd helped Overlea in the past, but that was the extent of his knowledge.

Everyone knew him as the Unaffected Earl. Ashford didn't have to look around to know that every eye in the room was on them. This man held a unique position in society. Ashford didn't know why, having been away from England for so long, but he did know that every man in that room would kill to be in Ashford's seat.

He'd faced countless men across a battlefield, however. It would take more than this man's icy stare to unnerve him.

"I assume introductions aren't necessary?"

"Of course not," Ashford said. "To what do I owe this honor?"

One blond brow lifted. While the man's expression remained impassive, Ashford got the impression he was amused.

"You're not easily intimidated. Good."

Ashford shrugged. "I would have made a poor soldier if I allowed myself to be cowed by a steady gaze."

Brantford smiled.

Ashford hadn't been aware of the quiet that had fallen around them until conversation picked up again at this small display of emotion from the man opposite him. "Do you always have this effect?"

"It can be useful to cultivate a certain aloofness."

An aloofness that Ashford knew had been tempered when the man married. He might not have met the Earl of Brantford before today, but he'd heard the stories during his brief time back in England. And those stories all said this man was clearly in love with his wife.

Honestly, it was as though everyone even remotely within Lowenbrock's circle of acquaintance could be said to be happily married. Given the rarity of such marriages among the ton, it was enough to make one wonder.

It also gave him hope for his own prospects with Mary.

"I'm here to speak to you about Miss Trenton."

For a moment Ashford wondered if the man had read his thoughts. "I wasn't aware you were acquainted with her."

Brantford raised a shoulder. "I'm not, but my wife is. And she is concerned."

Annoyance flared to life within him. It was one thing for his friends to ask him about his intentions, but this man was a stranger. "I can assure you that my intentions are honorable."

"So the two of you have reached an understanding?"

Unmistakable heat prickled under his collar, but he ignored the sensation. "It hasn't been formalized, but I hope to remedy that soon."

Brantford's eyes bored into him, but he refused to flinch. Nor would he rush to break the silence.

"Miss Trenton is staying with Lowenbrock and his wife."

It wasn't a question. Ashford nodded.

"Which means," Brantford continued, "that they will not allow her to be taken advantage of."

Ashford raised a brow. "How can you be sure

about that? Perhaps the man is a scoundrel who doesn't care about protecting Miss Trenton."

Brantford was silent for a moment, and then he laughed. It was short, but the sound was enough to gain the attention of those around them who weren't even trying to hide the fact they were attempting to overhear their conversation. One man turned his chair and leaned toward them, but a single glance from Brantford was enough to have him standing and excusing himself.

"Let us get to the point," Ashford said, tired of being under this man's scrutiny and having every eye in the room on him. "I can assure you that I do not have any ill intentions toward Miss Trenton. We are not yet betrothed, but I'm hoping that will soon change."

Brantford leaned forward and lowered his voice further. "You should know that Lady Fairbanks is going to be a problem."

Ashford shook his head. "You needn't fear for Miss Trenton's future."

"While I'm glad to hear that, you should know the woman is making moves to ruin her sister's chances for happiness."

Dread pooled in his veins. "In what way?"

"To begin, you should speak to Lowenbrock. Since Miss Trenton is under his protection, it won't raise any eyebrows for him to make arrangements to have his solicitor secure her inheritance."

Ashford swore.

"Quite so," Brantford said. "Right now Lady Fairbanks is just making inquiries, but I fear what else she might do. And I promised my wife that I would make sure no ill befalls her friend. From any quarter."

Ashford took heed of the warning. This was not a man one wanted as an enemy. "I'll speak to John. Make no mistake, we'll ensure Miss Trenton is protected. But you should know that I wouldn't care if she didn't have a penny to her name. I have no need of her dowry."

Brantford examined him for another moment before rising from his chair. "I'll let you get back to your friends then."

CHAPTER 22

Lowenbrock and Cranston joined him moments later. The latter asked the question that everyone in the room wanted to know the answer to.

"What on earth was all that about?"

Ashford turned to Lowenbrock. "Is there anyone in London Miss Trenton isn't friends with?"

His friend raised a shoulder. "I wasn't aware she was friends with Brantford, but I do know that his wife has been to the house. She's great friends with my sister Catherine."

"And apparently with Miss Trenton."

Cranston clapped him on the shoulder. "It was nice knowing you, old boy."

Ashford's jaw tightened in exasperation as he knocked the man's hand away. "I'll get to our conversation in a moment, but first, as I was saying before that interruption… Miss Trenton and I came to an agreement at the start of the season that our courtship would be for show only. But things have changed."

Cranston groaned. "Here we go."

Lowenbrock grinned. "Changed for the better?"

It was impossible to keep his own smile at bay. "I've developed feelings for her. Feelings that I believe are reciprocated."

"I thought you were above such nonsense," Cranston said with a wince.

Ashford swept his hand from Lowenbrock to the group of men sitting at the bow window. "I present to you proof that love can be very real."

"I don't think anyone is surprised that Sir Galahad found his fair maiden and is living happily ever after. I can't speak for the other men except to say that the odds are against either of us finding such happiness."

Ashford tilted his head to Lowenbrock's brother-in-law and his friends again, and Cranston huffed out an impatient breath.

"Well, it's about time you've come to your senses," Lowenbrock said. "But I must admit you've seemed distant with Miss Trenton of late, and she appears to be unhappy. I expected you to say the two of you were breaking off the ruse."

Ashford frowned. "I was trying to be circumspect. To let her know that my intentions are honorable."

Cranston blew out a harsh breath. "I can't believe

I'm about to say this, but being distant isn't the way to win a woman's heart."

Ashford crossed his arms over his chest. "I'm not sure I'd trust your advice on the matter."

"I was young once and foolishly gave my heart to a woman." Cranston shook his head. "It was many years ago, and after she stomped all over it, I enlisted. The last place I wanted to be was in England after seeing her wedding announcement to another."

Ashford's heart went out to the man. He couldn't imagine how devastated he'd be if he learned Mary had accepted another man's proposal.

"You never told us," Lowenbrock said.

"That I was young and stupid? That was hardly something I wanted to share." Cranston leaned forward in his chair. "Setting aside all this talk about love, I think Miss Trenton has a good head on her shoulders. She has wit and is quite attractive."

Ashford ground his teeth together, and Cranston laughed. "If what Sir Galahad says is correct, you should go talk to her now before she sets her heart on another man."

He winced just thinking about that eventuality. "I need to speak to her as soon as possible. But first—" He turned to Lowenbrock. "We need to see your solicitor."

CHAPTER 23

Mary paced the floor of her bedroom, trying to decide what to do. One week had passed since that wonderful night out in the gazebo. Ashford had shown her physical delight she'd never even imagined—despite what Amelia had assured her. Rapture made all the more powerful because she'd come to care for the man. To love him.

She had to speak to Amelia. Ashford would be joining them for dinner again tonight, and she needed her friend's advice. She was tempted to go to her friend's bedroom but quickly discarded the notion. Lowenbrock was home, and they might be sharing a private moment.

Instead, she penned a quick note and asked a maid to deliver it to the marchioness.

She didn't expect to find Amelia at her bedroom

door minutes later but was grateful she wouldn't have to wait.

She sank onto the edge of her bed. "I think Ashford has changed his mind about courting me."

Amelia took a seat next to her. "Nonsense. The man is smitten with you. Everyone can see it… *I* could see it last summer when you were both at the estate."

A ghost of a smile touched Mary's lips as memories filled her mind. She'd liked Ashford then but not romantically. She'd thought a man like him would never be interested in her. She should have remembered that their courtship was only pretend, but instead she'd allowed herself to get carried away.

"Our courtship isn't real."

"So you've told me. But while the man may have started out thinking it was only pretend, that's no longer true. You told me he kissed you."

Heat touched her cheeks. "And perhaps a little bit more."

Amelia's brows drew together. "Do you care for him?"

Mary wanted to say no, but she wouldn't lie. Neither to Amelia nor to herself. "It started out as friendship. It was fun playing the role, and I'll admit that it amused me to see Edwina go a little insane at the possibility I would marry the man she'd dreamed of having for herself when she was a young girl."

"And what do you feel now? Friendship is a great place from which to start."

Mary closed her eyes and let out a breath before meeting her friend's gaze. "I've discovered that I love him."

Amelia's grin threatened to split her face. "I knew it."

"But he's been pulling away this past week. Since… the masquerade. I think he's changed his mind."

Amelia drew her into a tight hug, then released her. "Don't give up on him yet."

Mary wanted to tell her friend that not every story has a happy ending. Amelia had gotten one herself, but Mary didn't think the same would happen for her.

"I'm worried about dinner tonight. I have a feeling that matters will finally come to an end."

Amelia looked like she wanted to say something but shook her head and pulled Mary to her feet. "You were there for me when things went awry with John, so know that I'll always be there for you. I'm telling you to have faith… and to believe in the possibility of a happy ending for yourself."

Mary wanted that more than she'd ever wanted anything.

~

When she and Amelia made their way downstairs, she could hear male voices coming from the drawing room. Ashford and Lord Lowenbrock.

She didn't realize she'd stopped until Amelia took hold of her hand and gave it a squeeze. Mary took a deep breath before nodding to her friend and continuing to the drawing room.

Ashford's gaze locked on hers with an intensity that had her steps faltering. He murmured something to Amelia's husband before crossing the room toward her. Mary sensed her friend going to her husband's side, but she only had eyes for the man standing before her now. The man with the power to make her whole or break her apart.

"Can we speak in private?" His deep voice sent a shiver of awareness through her. It was the same tone he'd used when they were intimate that night in the gazebo. She hadn't heard it since then.

She was acutely aware of her friends' eyes on them. She wanted to believe she could have this… That she could have him. But fear had her bracing for the worst.

Perhaps she could put this off for one more day. It was cowardly, but she couldn't face the reality that her all-too-brief time with this man was over. "I'm sure that anything you wish to say to me can be said right here."

His gaze roamed over her face, and she let out a breath of relief. He would let the matter drop now.

But instead, he straightened, and dread settled in the pit of her stomach like a lead weight.

"I love you, Mary Trenton."

Her breath came out in a whoosh, and she realized she was gaping at him. "You do?"

His gaze softened, and the corners of his mouth turned up. "I'd hoped to do this in private, but…" He dropped to one knee. "Say you'll accept my suit. I can't bear the thought of being without you."

She couldn't believe this was actually happening. Ashford loved her. They were no longer just pretending. "I love you too. So much. But I fear I might be dreaming again."

Ashford rose to his feet and tugged her into his arms. "If you're dreaming, then so am I. But you still haven't told me if you'll have me."

She brought one hand to his cheek. "Yes."

He gave a whoop, one that was echoed by their audience, and swung her around.

Laughing, she leaned up to press a light kiss on his lips, wishing now that she'd agreed to his request for privacy.

He leaned down and spoke into her ear, his low voice and the warmth of his breath causing gooseflesh to rise on her arms. "I'll be back for you later. I think it's time I showed you everything I was holding back before."

She pulled back and stared up at him. The look in his eyes reminded her of that night in the gazebo.

"After dinner. I'm sure Amelia and Lord Lowenbrock will look the other way. I know they were together before their marriage as well."

He drew both of her hands up to his mouth and dropped a kiss onto each one. Mary shivered at the sensation of his warm lips against her gloveless fingers. His gaze met hers, one corner of his mouth lifting. But all too soon, he stepped back and drew her hand into the crook of his arm. Together, they turned to face their rapt audience.

Amelia swept her into an embrace. "Didn't I say that you and Lord Ashford made a perfect pair?"

Mary laughed. "You'll never let me forget this, will you?"

Amelia grinned at her. "Perhaps in a few years' time."

Lowenbrock dipped his head. "You have a good man there. I know he'll make you happy."

Ashford smiled down at her. "I'll certainly spend the rest of my life trying."

CHAPTER 24

There was much good-natured teasing aimed at him and Mary during dinner. Apparently they were the last to know they'd make a match. Even Cranston had told Lowenbrock it was only a matter of time.

His mother and sister were going to be ecstatic. But before they announced their betrothal to his family and to the world, Ashford needed to get Mary alone. He planned to ruin her for anyone else… just as she had ruined him.

When the dessert plate was taken away, he cast a frustrated glance at Mary. He was at a loss as to how exactly he was going to go about this. He couldn't exactly come out and tell Lowenbrock he was going upstairs with his houseguest. Mary was a gently bred young woman, and they weren't wed yet.

As she'd done many times now, Mary came to his

rescue. "It's such a lovely evening. I think Lord Ashford and I will go for a walk in the gardens."

Lowenbrock's wife did a very poor job of trying to hide her grin. "Of course. It was so nice of you to join us this evening. I'm sure we'll see you more often now?"

"Until we can finalize our wedding plans, I'll consider this my second home."

Lowenbrock nodded, but it was clear the man was hiding a grin. "We'll say our goodbyes then. Have a nice evening."

Mary took his arm, and together they made their way to the back of the house. It appeared that they were going to do this in the gazebo after all. It wasn't what he'd planned, but this time he wasn't going to stop until he made this woman his.

Mary tugged him to the left, and he followed her down a side hall, away from the garden doors. She stopped before a wall panel and pressed against it. He grinned when the panel slid back to reveal a servant's stairway.

This woman was brilliant. She dropped her hold on his arm, and he followed her up the dark staircase, careful to close the secret panel behind him. Thankfully, they didn't run into any servants along the way. They would know what happened this evening, of course—the servants always knew what happened under the roofs of the houses in which they served.

But that didn't mean he wanted to flaunt what they were about to do in front of them.

When they emerged on the second floor, he reached for her hand, enjoying the way her fingers felt clasped within his. Her room was the first doorway on the right.

They slipped into the room without a word, and he turned to lock the door. Nothing was going to stop him tonight, but first he needed to make sure she was ready for what they were about to do.

When he turned, she flowed into his arms as though she was meant to be there and raised her face. Powerless to hold back, he kissed her. She made a soft sigh of contentment, and he wanted nothing more than to drown in her.

He raised his head and gazed down at her. When she opened her eyes, they were cloudy with desire.

"I need to know you're fine with proceeding."

By way of answer, she started to undo his cravat. He waited as she untied the simple knot he preferred and drew the linen from his neck. Her eyes dropped to the top of his shirt where the fabric was now gaping open.

"Mary…"

She took one step back and turned away from him. He realized his breathing was already heavy and they'd only shared one all-too-brief kiss.

She looked back at him over her shoulder. "I'm

going to need some assistance with the buttons. Unless you'd rather leave so I can summon my maid?"

That was all the answer he needed. He started at the top, fumbling slightly with buttons that seemed far too delicate for his large hands. He leaned in close to her ear as he worked. "How close is your hosts' bedchamber?"

A shiver went through her. "They are all the way on the other end of the hall."

Not far enough for his liking but he would make this work. When he reached the end of the row of buttons, he undid the laces of her stays for good measure and then began to remove the pins from her hair. The light brown mass fell across her upper back like a curtain.

Content with his handiwork, he dropped his arms and waited to see what she would do next.

Mary turned, her dark blue dress now loose around her shoulders. She took her lower lip between her teeth, and he didn't miss the way she drew in a deep breath before she allowed the dress to fall down her body and stepped out of it. Her corset followed, and she stood before him wearing only her chemise.

Of course she was nervous. He would do whatever it took to alleviate her fear. He shrugged out of his tailcoat and began to unbutton his waistcoat. She followed the movement with her eyes. When her tongue dipped out to lick at her lower lip, his control snapped. He tossed the garments aside, not caring where they landed, and dragged her back into his arms.

He'd seen her wearing less, her breasts exposed to the night air, but he'd been fully clothed then. The feel of her against him, the thin fabric her chemise and his shirt the only barrier between them, felt better than he'd imagined. Because this was Mary and every other woman paled in comparison.

They met in a heated kiss that seemed to go on forever. But his patience was now at an end.

He removed his shirt, impatient to do away with the rest of his clothing.

Her mouth dropped open. "Oh my," she said, reaching out to rest a hand on his chest. Her other hand followed, and he had to grit his teeth as she explored his chest, his arms, and good Lord, his abdomen. For a moment he wondered if she was going to explore further.

"I don't know what to do. You're going to have to show me."

He swooped down for a short kiss. Much as he wanted to ask her to strip down to her bare skin, he knew she wasn't ready for that. Perhaps next time… He had to push that thought away if he hoped to go slowly.

"Get onto the bed. I'll join you in a moment."

With a nod, she did as he asked. He sat on the bed next to her and gazed down, searching for any hint of doubt. When he saw none, he dropped a kiss onto her forehead. "I'm going to remove the rest of my clothing now. It's fine if you watch me."

He half expected her to look away, but of course, this was Mary and she was never one to shy away from a challenge. Her curiosity must have overtaken her trepidation because she raised herself onto her elbows to do just that.

He removed his boots first before standing. Heat colored her cheeks as she watched him undo the buttons of his trousers. He turned away before peeling them down his legs and stepping out of them.

He left them on the floor and turned to face her. He was already hard, and he watched as Mary's gaze traveled down to that part of him. Heat colored her cheeks, and she met his gaze again. He lowered himself to sit beside her again.

"You know what is going to happen now?"

Mary nodded. "Amelia felt the need to educate me on the matter."

He cupped her chin, using his thumb to rub against her lower lip. "I need to ask you one more question before we proceed."

"I'm sure about this."

He let out a small bark of laughter and gave her another quick kiss. "I wouldn't have disrobed if I thought you had any doubts. No, I need to ask you about your monthly courses."

She closed her eyes. "Why?"

He knew this wasn't a subject women liked to discuss with men. "Look at me."

She opened one eye, then the other, with a sigh. When she didn't speak, he continued. "We need to be careful that you don't fall with child before we're wed. I've… learned a few things about how a woman's courses might affect the likelihood of that happening. Are you regular? Do you know when you're likely to bleed again?"

She swallowed and he waited. Finally she said, "I've only ever spoken about this with my maid. I can't believe I'm having this conversation with you."

He waited. He had no intention of stopping unless she asked him to, but her answer would tell him whether he'd be able to finish inside her as he very much wanted to.

"They're due to arrive in a few days' time. What does that mean?"

He traced his thumb along her jaw, then moved to cup the back of her head. "It means there won't be enough time for my seed to take root within you."

She gave her head a small shake. "I don't even want to know how you've come about this knowledge."

Instead of answering, he kissed her again. When she wound her arms around his neck, he was lost. He shifted until he was lying on the bed next to her and drew her against him. He wanted nothing more than to rip her chemise from her body, but it served as a reminder that he needed to go slowly.

He flipped them around so she was over him, and she let out a small yelp at the unexpected movement.

She drew back, a small vee between her brows. "I thought the man—"

He stopped her question with a finger to her lips. "In time, my sweet."

Her brow smoothed and she kissed him again.

He took advantage of their positions to begin tugging the chemise down, baring first her shoulders, then her breasts. Then he started the agonizingly slow journey of kissing down her jaw, her throat, her shoulder, and finally took one breast into his mouth.

Mary let out a small sound of contentment and placed her hands on his cheeks. She liked this, and he was content to draw out her pleasure, suckling on one breast and then the other.

She made a soft sound of frustration, and he stopped to look up at her. "My arms are caught."

He laughed softly at seeing how her chemise was working to constrict her movements. "Let's free you then."

She grinned down at him, and together they freed her arms from the fine linen undergarment. He rolled her onto her back then and dragged the fabric down the rest of her, his eyes tracing over every inch of her body along the way.

"Are you just going to keep staring at me?"

He gave his head a small shake. "What would my lady have me do?"

She took that bottom lip between her teeth again, and this time he did groan.

"Kiss me? Touch me?" She punctuated her words with her own caresses, drawing her hands down his chest before stopping at his waist.

He shifted, lowering his body over hers again. "As you desire."

There was a hunger inside him that he was powerless to hold back. But he didn't need to because Mary met that passion, her tongue surging into his mouth and her hands lowering to cup his backside.

He couldn't wait. He wanted to, but he didn't have that much strength inside him. He reached down to her folds, satisfaction and lust surging in his veins when he found she was already wet for him.

"I'm going to worship you with my mouth later," he said against her lips. "But right now I need to make you mine."

She shook her head. "I'm already yours." She opened her legs, allowing him to settle between her thighs.

This woman was going to be the death of him. How had he become so fortunate? "I love you, Mary Trenton."

He sank into her quickly, hoping that doing so would lessen the duration of pain. And from the way her face tightened, it was clear he'd hurt her.

He stilled and began to kiss her again, hoping to distract her while he allowed her body time to adjust to him.

She threaded her fingers into his hair and kissed him back.

"I'm so sorry I hurt you," he said after some time had passed. Probably not long enough, but he wasn't sure how much longer he could hold back. Every part of his body was screaming at him to move.

She looked deep into his eyes. "Make love to me, Ashford."

With a groan, he did just that, starting slowly. When she wrapped her legs around his hips and started to thrust back, he lost all control. Somehow he lasted long enough for her to reach her peak, taking joy in the way her head arched backward. He had the presence of mind to cover her mouth, which turned out to be a good thing because his Mary was a screamer.

He followed, burying his face in her neck and groaning into the warm skin there.

He stayed that way, breathing harshly against her while she continued to twine her fingers through his hair. She didn't complain about his weight, but he knew he couldn't stay on top of her for long.

Finally he rolled to the side. They lay face-to-face, their arms still wrapped around each other.

"That was quite nice," Mary said.

He let out a bark of laughter, and this time it was

Mary's turn to cover his mouth. Her eyes danced with mirth.

He kissed her palm, and she slid her hand along his cheek. "You are an original, Miss Trenton."

He moved onto his back, contentment settling over him when his betrothed rested her head on his shoulder. He'd have to get dressed and leave soon, but not just yet. He wanted to enjoy this moment a while longer.

He rubbed circles along her back as their heated skin began to cool, affection pulling at his heart when she hummed with contentment.

"I met with my solicitor," he said.

She dropped a kiss onto his chest. "About?"

"You. Our marriage contract."

She looked up at him. "I still have the funds my father left me for my dowry."

"I know. But I wanted to make sure that money stayed in your name, for your use."

The way her eyes widened told him he'd surprised her. "But it's customary—"

He stopped her question with a kiss. "It may be customary, but it isn't required. You spent far too many years subject to your sister's whims. I couldn't take away the small measure of freedom you've managed to gain. While I hope that wherever you choose to go, I'll be at your side, I didn't want you to feel as though you were completely reliant on me."

"So we don't need to wed?" The laughter in her

eyes told him she was trying to get a rise out of him. It worked.

He flipped her onto her back and rose up over her. "Perhaps I need to give you further inducement to stay with me."

He started to kiss his way down her body again, intent on wringing so much pleasure from her that she'd never again talk about leaving him, even in jest.

EPILOGUE

June 1817

Ashford took in the groups of people present that afternoon as he and Mary strolled through Hyde Park. There was no need today to stay perched above the crowds on his phaeton. The betrothal announcement had already run in all the newspapers. Gone were their days of trying to put on a show for everyone.

The season would be drawing to a close soon, and it seemed as though everyone was at the park, intent on enjoying the last weeks before they all returned to the country. The day was perfect—sunny but not yet oppressively hot.

It was almost impossible to believe that in one month's time, right before everyone left London, he would be a married man. Even more difficult to believe was the fact he was counting down the days with eagerness.

Only three months had passed since he'd declared his intention to court Mary Trenton by taking her on a drive through Hyde Park. Now he couldn't wait to bind her to him forever.

"Lord Cranston!" Mary exclaimed as his friend pulled his own phaeton to the side and jumped down from the high perch with ease. "I didn't expect to see you here this afternoon."

Cranston took hold of her hand and bowed over it before taking a step back. "I thought I'd come to ensure this scoundrel was treating you well."

Ashford didn't even care that one of his best friends was blatantly flirting with his intended. He trusted the man without question, even if he was a scoundrel.

Together they continued their walk.

"I can scarce believe that in one month's time I will be Lady Ashford. I must admit, Lord Lowenbrock has been a saint. Amelia has all manner of people coming into the house for my trousseau. And then there are the preparations at Ashford's home for the wedding breakfast. Who would have thought that a simple meal would require so much planning?"

Ashford squeezed Mary's hand where it was resting in the crook of his elbow. "If my mother is being difficult, please let me know. I'm a viscount, not the Prince Regent. I don't know why she keeps changing her mind about what's going to be served and which cutlery we'll be using. And the guest list keeps growing. I'm beginning to think we should have set the date for after everyone quits town."

Mary met his gaze. "I'm sure the next month will fly by."

He didn't realize they'd stopped and were standing there, gazing at one another and no doubt putting on quite the display, until Cranston groaned.

"Why am I even here? Perhaps I should see if there's anyone else I can speak to where I won't feel decidedly *de trop*."

Mary blushed. "We apologize for making you feel unwelcome."

Ashford let out a chuckle at the way his friend was gazing up and down the walk, exaggerating his efforts to see who was present inside the carriages that were slowly driving past them.

They walked in companionable silence for almost a full minute before Mary exclaimed, "Oh look, there's Lady Holbrook. I met her the other day while out with Amelia and she seems delightful. I would love to become better acquainted."

Ashford didn't miss the way his friend stiffened beside him. He watched as Cranston followed Mary's gaze. When his eyes landed on Lady Holbrook, a muscle jumped in his tense jaw.

Mary glared at Cranston. "She may be a widow,

but I like her a great deal. Promise me that you won't trifle with her and break her heart."

They stopped walking again when Cranston froze in place. Ashford's eyes narrowed as he came to a realization. He leaned toward his friend and said in a low voice, for Cranston's ears only, "Is that…?"

Cranston offered a terse nod.

Ashford started to turn Mary around. "You can introduce us at a later date. But for now we should return to the carriage. If the road becomes any more clogged with traffic, we'll be here forever."

When Cranston didn't join them, it took a great deal of restraint not to turn around to see what his friend was doing.

He helped Mary back into the carriage. When he saw her too-astute gaze was fixed on Cranston, he let out a soft breath and turned around.

His friend was still staring at Lady Holbrook, but after several more seconds, he turned and stalked back to his own carriage, his long strides eating up the distance.

Mary sighed. "It would seem he's already had his way with her. I swear, the way that man dallies is positively scandalous. I only hope he's restrained himself to widows."

Ashford climbed onto the bench seat of the phaeton and took hold of the ribbons. With a soft command, the team began to move forward slowly.

Finally they turned onto the main street outside of Hyde Park.

Once there was no danger of being overheard, he explained. "They knew one another years ago, before he purchased his commission. From what Cranston told me recently after having one too many drinks, he'd wanted to marry her."

Mary let out a soft gasp. "What happened?"

He figured he might as well tell her. If she became friends with Lady Holbrook, it was likely Mary would hear some version of what had happened from the woman. "Her father didn't approve of the match, and so they'd planned to elope. But at the last minute, she broke his heart and married someone else with her father's approval. Apparently she was very cruel when Cranston confronted her."

Mary's hands flew to her chest. "That's terrible. Is that why he's so… free with his attention to other women?"

Ashford found his own chest tightening as he thought of his friend's heartache. "Not everyone is as happy as we are."

"I was hoping to befriend Lady Holbrook. She struck me as being refreshingly honest, which is a rarity among the ton. And she's a widow now. Maybe if I discover what happened all those years ago, we can help them."

He cast a sideways glance at her, his eyes narrowing.

"Don't look at me that way. We both know that women have little choice in whom they wed. Now that she has gained a measure of freedom, they may be able to find love again."

"You've forgotten the part about her being cruel to him."

She winced. "I was hoping that was an exaggeration. Perhaps it just felt as though she were being cruel."

He shook his head. "We should let the matter drop. Nothing good can come from digging up past hurts."

"But—"

"If Cranston wanted to pursue the matter, he would have approached her here, where he could test the waters in public. I think it was clear to both of us that he has no desire to renew the acquaintance."

Mary folded her arms across her chest. "What if she's the one woman who can make him happy? He hasn't shown any interest—*lasting* interest—in another woman."

"Even if that were true, I doubt he'd be open to the possibility." Mary opened her mouth to reply, but he continued. "Make no mistake, I love the man like a brother and would do anything for him. And I have, in fact, risked my life for him. But I don't think he'll ever forgive her."

"So he doesn't plan to wed?"

He'd never thought about Cranston's prospects.

Had never really thought about his own save for the knowledge that he'd wed sometime in the distant future. "I couldn't say. But I do know that if he does decide to wed, it will be a practical union with someone he thinks will fulfill the role of his baroness. Love won't enter into the equation."

Mary didn't say anything further, but the way she gazed off into the distance told him she was considering his words. He only hoped that the practical side of his future wife's nature would win out over the romantic he'd come to know in the past few months. If his warning didn't convince her that any attempt at matchmaking would end in failure, she'd find out for herself soon enough.

He'd just have to redouble his efforts to keep Mary's thoughts on him and not on matchmaking. Ashford grinned as he imagined all the ways he could accomplish that goal.

I hope you enjoyed reading Mary and Ashford's story. If you want more, there is a bonus epilogue available! Sign up for my newsletter here to get access to my bonus content!

Cranston and Lady Holbrook's story is next in *The Baron's Return.*

Turn the page for an excerpt from *A Viscount for Christmas*, which is book 1 in my new CHRISTMAS SCANDALS series.

EXCERPT—A VISCOUNT FOR CHRISTMAS

An unexpected Christmas gift…

When Viscount Isaac Thornton returns home for his mother's annual Christmas gathering, the last thing he expects to find is a beautiful woman sleeping in his bed. But Celia isn't yet another woman trying to trap him into marriage. She's his younger sister's best friend and now she's all grown up.

Celia Rowland outgrew the infatuation she had for Thornton years ago. When a misunderstanding means she's been compromised, her mother insists they get married.

One house party and two people trying to escape a forced wedding who just might get the Christmas gift they didn't know they wanted.

December 1816

It was past midnight when Viscount Isaac Thornton reached his estate in Surrey. He'd been on horseback for several hours. Normally the ride wasn't a difficult one, but with the cold temperatures, he'd needed to stop frequently to change horses.

Filled with a bone-deep fatigue that emphasized the unwelcome fact he'd recently passed his thirtieth birthday, all he wanted to do was sleep. He wasn't looking forward to the next week. His mother's yearly Christmas party would be yet another opportunity for her to remind him he needed to settle down and produce an heir. He couldn't avoid his mother's matchmaking altogether, but he could limit the duration of his suffering. Which was why he'd originally planned to arrive the day before Christmas and depart again the day after the holiday.

She'd successfully thwarted those plans with the greatest weapon in her arsenal—guilt. He'd received her letter that afternoon. In it, she told him how much she looked forward to spending quality time with him. She'd gone on to inform him that his two younger sisters, who lived in the north of England, wouldn't be attending because the roads were impassable after a heavy snowfall that hadn't reached Surrey. To alleviate what he knew would be her very real disappointment, he'd changed his plans and set out to join her when her house party would still be in full swing.

If he were being honest with himself, London had become tedious of late, especially after his friends and most of his acquaintances quit town and headed to their own estates for the holiday season. His mother's letter was a convenient excuse to return home earlier than planned.

He apologized to the sleepy groom who greeted him moments after he reached the stables. He was relieved to discover the manor was quiet as he made his way to the front door on foot. Perhaps his mother hadn't invited that many people this year.

But even as the thought occurred to him, he knew it was a futile wish. Christmas was his mother's favorite time of the year, and she was known for her winter house parties. This year wouldn't be any different.

He was surprised when the front door was opened by Saunders, their butler, and not a footman. He'd hoped to surprise his mother, but apparently she knew him too well. She'd expected him to set out for Surrey after receiving her letter.

He greeted the older man and handed him his hat and greatcoat, barely taking in the evergreen boughs and festive decorations that tastefully highlighted the fact the festive season was upon them. He'd started toward the stairs when Saunders coughed discreetly.

Thornton turned to face him.

"Your mother wishes to speak with you, my lord."

Thornton frowned. No doubt she wanted to tell him who she'd invited and why he should pay particular attention to each one of them. He'd just arrived, and already the matchmaking had begun.

He nodded. "I'll speak to her in the morning."

"She insisted—"

Thornton wouldn't take his annoyance out on this man whom he'd known since he was a child. Saunders was merely carrying out Lady Thornton's instructions.

"I already know what she wants to speak to me about."

"But—"

"Good night, Saunders. I'll speak to my mother first thing in the morning. And get some rest yourself." The man had no doubt been awake since dawn.

Before Saunders could say another word, Thornton turned and made his way upstairs.

He didn't ring for his valet when he reached his bedroom, too tired to care about the lecture the man would deliver tomorrow as he tossed his clothes onto a chair.

*-It was dark, but he didn't need to light a candle. He made his way to the bed and slid under the covers. His eyes were closing when a small movement on the other side of the bed chased away his fatigue.

He was imagining things. Or, more likely, he'd already fallen asleep and was dreaming. Still, he was wide awake now. He rolled over and narrowed his gaze on the other side of the bed, where he could see a small bundle wrapped in his blankets.

In retrospect, he should have sprung from the bed and thrown on his clothes. But he didn't really expect to find anything, and so he pulled back the bedsheets. It took his befuddled senses several seconds to process the fact he wasn't alone.

Someone was already asleep in his bed—a woman, to be precise. She lay with her back to him, and he could only stare at her for what felt like the longest minute of his life.

His fumbling in the dark hadn't caused her to move, so she must be asleep. His gaze took in the long golden hair that covered most of her back. Unbound, which surprised him. Unable to stop himself, he gazed down to where her hair ended just above the curve of her hip, which was covered in a white nightgown. The blankets covered the rest of her, and he resisted the temptation to drag them down even farther.

Casting aside the temptation to see whether she would be well endowed, he shifted onto his back and slung a hand over his eyes. He doubted very much that his mother had arranged this woman as a welcome-home present for him. She'd probably wanted to warn him that she had given away his room to another guest.

Which meant he had to dress again and find a servant to lead him to a room that was unoccupied.

He rose to a seating position with a muffled groan. He thought he'd been quiet, but the shifting of his weight must have woken the woman, because she rolled onto her back. Her eyes blinked open, and she let out a sleepy yawn. And then a scream.

That should have had him moving with alacrity, gathering up his clothes and escaping into the dressing room. But his brief glimpse at her form before she'd pulled up the bedcovers caused him to freeze. In the dim light, he could see that she was, indeed, well endowed.

Why did these things never happen to him under better circumstances? For it was clear now that he wasn't dreaming. If he were, she would have beckoned him to her with open arms. Instead, the woman in his bed had gathered up the blankets and held them to her breast like a shield.

"What are you doing here? You must leave at once!"

Yes, this wasn't a dream. "This is my bedroom."

Her mouth gaped open before she closed it with a snap. "You're not suggesting…" She took a deep breath and began again. "We can sort out this mess tomorrow morning. But a gentleman would leave without question and find another bedroom."

He couldn't resist teasing her. "Perhaps I'm not a gentleman."

She sputtered, speechless. Taking pity on her, he slipped from the bed with a soft curse.

"I don't know why you're upset. I'm the injured party here."

Something about the prim tone of her voice seemed familiar. He strode to the window and drew back the curtains to let in some of the moonlight. Then he returned to the bed—the side the woman occupied—and leaned forward to examine her. She leaned back with a squawk.

His eyes roamed over her face. Blond hair, blue eyes… she could have been anyone. But then he saw the small mole at the corner of her right eye.

"Celia Rowland?"

She huffed out an impatient breath. "That's Miss Rowland to you, my lord. Now will you please leave?"

He had to give her credit. Another woman might have given in to a fit of vapors at finding a man in her bed, but not Celia. He remembered her only as his youngest sister's friend. She'd been pretty, and he remembered finding her sweet, but she'd also been much too young for him the last time he'd seen her. He couldn't deny that she'd grown into a beautiful young woman.

He didn't miss the way her gaze dipped to his bare chest and couldn't hold back his smirk. "Like what you see?"

Her eyes met his again. "I was merely—"

"Admiring my fine form? Wondering if you'd asked me to leave too soon?"

She let out an impatient huff. "Is it your intention to compromise me?"

And that's when the reality of the situation settled into place. His understanding came too late, however, because the bedroom door was thrown open.

BOOKS BY SUZANNA MEDEIROS

Dear Stranger

Forbidden in February (A Year Without a Duke multi-author series)

Anthologies:

The Novellas: A Collection

Hathaway Heirs: Books 1-4

Landing a Lord: Books 1-3

Landing a Lord series:

Dancing with the Duke

Loving the Marquess

Beguiling the Earl

The Unaffected Earl

The Unsuitable Duke

The Unexpected Marquess

The Unwilling Viscount

The Baron's Return (Coming next!)

Christmas Scandals series:

A Viscount for Christmas

A Highwayman for Christmas (Christmas 2022)

Hathaway Heirs series:

Lady Hathaway's Proposal

Lord Hathaway's Bride

Captain Hathaway's Dilemma

Miss Hathaway's Wish

For more information please visit the author's website:
https://www.suzannamedeiros.com/books/

ABOUT SUZANNA

USA Today bestselling author Suzanna Medeiros was born and raised in Toronto, Canada. Her love for the written word led her to pursue a degree in English Literature from the University of Toronto. She went on to earn a Bachelor of Education degree but graduated at a time when no teaching jobs were available. After working at a number of interesting places, including a federal inquiry, a youth probation office, and the Office of the Fire Marshal of Ontario, she decided to pursue her first love—writing.

Suzanna is married to her own hero and is the proud mother of twin daughters. She is an avowed romantic who enjoys spending her days writing love stories.

She would like to thank her parents for showing her that love at first sight and happily ever after really do exist.

To learn about Suzanna Medeiros's future books, sign up for her newsletter:
https://www.suzannamedeiros.com/newsletter

Visit her website:
https://www.suzannamedeiros.com

Or visit her on Facebook:
https://www.facebook.com/AuthorSuzannaMedeiros

Made in the USA
Monee, IL
26 June 2023

37596462R00139